P ID'S

IY

“Here, tak ; retort to sexual, racial, and historical oppression on a West Indian island, and perhaps elsewhere. . . . Kincaid does not say that Xuela is right. She says that you will not forget her. And she is right.”

—Richard Eder, *Los Angeles Times Book Review*

“A mother's love, or rather the absence or withdrawal or compromise of that love, lies at the heart of Jamaica Kincaid's fierce, incantatory novels. . . . The figure of the mother represents more than the woman who gave them life; she also represents the vanished and enduring past, a connection to earlier generations of women and blacks who endured the indignities of colonial and postcolonial oppression. . . . Writing in precise, lyrical prose that uses the repetition of images and words to build a musical rhythm, Ms. Kincaid conjures up the whole world of Dominica in all its beauty and casual cruelty . . . a world in which the ghosts of colonialism still haunt the relationships of contemporary women and men. In doing so she has written a powerful and disturbing book.”

—Michiko Kakutani, *New York Times Book Review*

JAMAICA KINCAID was born on the island of St. John's, Antigua. She is the author of *At the Bottom of the River* (1983), *Annie John* (1985), *Lucy* (1991), and the nonfiction work *A Small Place* (1988), all of which are available in Plume editions. She lives with her family in Vermont.

"What this 'autobiography' becomes is a document of deeds and consequences and mind-sets—meticulously structured chamber music in print—most comparable, perhaps, to Camus's *The Stranger*. . . . Jamaica Kincaid's own wealth, the dowry with which she faces the world, is a perfect prose style. It's fascinating to watch her take these several themes and elegantly, precisely, musically work them out to their inevitable conclusion." —Carolyn See, *Washington Post Book World*

"A powerful, disturbing novel." —*New York Daily News*

"Sensual, jarring observations." —*Library Journal*

"Brilliant, sensuous, mercilessly clear. . . . An eroticism of description pervades the novel. . . . Clothed in a language of power and beauty, Xuela's story is a testament of resistance: resistance to cruelty, political oppression, and the condition of being born without love, without comfort, without protection. Its intensity arises from the superhuman will of a person who has had to create herself by herself, depending on no one, who sees with eyes that no partiality has shaded."
—*Raleigh News and Observer*

"Kincaid's rhythms and the circularity of her thought patterns in language bring Gertrude Stein to mind. She is an eccentric and altogether impressive descendant." —*New York Review of Books*

"Mesmerizing, harrowing, richly metaphorical."
—*Publishers Weekly*

"Kincaid's prose is strong and erotic and powerful and austere." —*Fort Worth Star-Telegram*

"Through subtle, poetic meditations that continually question the boundaries between solitude and family, love and hate, black and white, colonialism and the colonized, Kincaid casts a lucid wash of language over Xuela's tragically barren life. The result is a narrative rife with lush imagery and sonorous biblical cadences that sharply contrast with the narrator's emotional rigidity and existential isolation." —*St. Petersburg Times*

"This is an unforgettable novel, the most powerful yet by one of our hemisphere's most essential writers."
—*Dallas Morning News*

ALSO BY JAMAICA KINCAID

*At the Bottom of the River*

*Annie John*

*A Small Place*

*Lucy*

# THE AUTOBIOGRAPHY OF MY MOTHER

*Jamaica Kincaid*

A PLUME BOOK

PLUME
Published by the Penguin Group
Penguin Books USA Inc., 375 Hudson Street,
New York, New York 10014, U.S.A.
Penguin Books Ltd, 27 Wrights Lane, London W8 5TZ, England
Penguin Books Australia Ltd, Ringwood, Victoria, Australia
Penguin Books Canada Ltd, 10 Alcorn Avenue,
Toronto, Ontario, Canada M4V 3B2
Penguin Books (N.Z.) Ltd, 182–190 Wairau Road, Auckland 10, New Zealand

Penguin Books Ltd, Registered Offices: Harmondsworth, Middlesex, England

Published by Plume, an imprint of Dutton Signet,
a division of Penguin Books USA Inc.
This is an authorized reprint of a hardcover edition published by Farrar, Straus and Giroux. For information address Farrar, Straus and Giroux, 19 Union Square West, New York, New York, 10003.

First Plume Printing, January, 1997
10 9 8 7 6 5



Part of this book appeared in a different form in *The New Yorker*.

REGISTERED TRADEMARK—MARCA REGISTRADA

LIBRARY OF CONGRESS CATALOGING-IN-PUBLICATION DATA
Kincaid, Jamaica.
The autobiography of my mother / Jamaica Kincaid.
p. cm.
ISBN 0-452-27466-4
1. Women—Dominica—Fiction. 2. Dominica—Fiction. I. Title.
PR9275.A583K5636 1997
813—dc20
96-29478
CIP

Printed in the United States of America



PUBLISHER'S NOTE
This is a work of fiction. Names, characters, places, and incidents either are the product of the author's imagination or are used fictitiously, and any resemblance to actual persons, living or dead, events, or locales is entirely coincidental.

FOR DEREK WALCOTT

My mother died at the moment I was born, and so for my whole life there was nothing standing between myself and eternity; at my back was always a bleak, black wind. I could not have known at the beginning of my life that this would be so; I only came to know this in the middle of my life, just at the time when I was no longer young and realized that I had less of some of the things I used to have in abundance and more of some of the things I had scarcely had at all. And this realization of loss and gain made me look backward and forward: at my beginning was this woman whose face I had never seen, but at my end was nothing, no one between me and the black room of the world. I came to feel that for my whole life I had been standing on a precipice, that my loss had made me vulnerable, hard, and helpless; on knowing this I became overwhelmed with sadness and shame and pity for myself.

When my mother died, leaving me a small child vulnerable to all the world, my father took me and placed me in the care of the same woman he paid to wash his clothes. It is possible that he emphasized to her the difference between the two bundles: one was his child, not his only child in the world but the only child he had with the only woman he had married so far; the other was his soiled clothes. He would have handled one more gently than the other, he would have given more careful instructions for the care of one over the other, he would have expected better care for one than the other, but which one I do not know, because he was a very vain man, his appearance was very important to him. That I was a burden to him, I know; that his soiled clothes were a burden to him, I know; that he did not know how to take care of me by himself, or how to clean his own clothes himself, I know.

He had lived in a very small house with my mother. He was poor, but it was not because he was good; he had not done enough bad things yet to get rich. This house was on a hill and he had walked down the hill balancing in one hand his child, in the other his clothes, and he had given them, bundle and child, to a woman. She was not a relative of his or of my mother's; her name was Eunice Paul, and she had six children already, the last one was still a baby. That was why she still had some milk in her breast to give to me, but in my mouth it tasted sour and I would not drink it. She lived in a house that was far from other houses, and from it there was a broad view of the sea and the mountains, and when I was irritable and unable to console myself, she would prop me up on pieces of old cloth and place me in the shade of a tree, and at the sight of that sea and those mountains, so unpitying, I would exhaust myself in tears.

Ma Eunice was not unkind: she treated me just the way she treated her own children—but this is not to say she was kind to her own children. In a place like this, brutality is the only real inheritance and cruelty is sometimes the only thing freely given. I did not like her, and I missed the face I had never seen; I looked over my shoulder to see if someone was coming, as if I were expecting someone to come, and Ma Eunice would ask me what I was looking for, at first as a joke, but when, after a time, I did not stop doing it, she thought it meant I could see spirits. I could not see spirits at all, I was just looking for that face, the face I would never see, even if I lived forever.

I never grew to love this woman my father left me with, this woman who was not unkind to me but who could not be kind because she did not know how—and perhaps I could not love her because I, too, did not know how. She fed me food forced through a sieve when I would not drink her milk and did not yet have teeth; when I grew teeth, the first thing I did was to sink them into her hand as she fed me. A small sound escaped her mouth then, more from surprise than from pain, and she knew this for what it was—my first act of ingratitude—and it put her on her guard against me for the rest of the time we knew each other.

Until I was four I did not speak. This did not cause anyone to lose a minute of happiness; there was no one who would have worried about it in any case. I knew I could speak, but I did not want to. I saw my father every fortnight, when he came to get his clean clothes. I never thought of him as coming to visit me; I thought of him as coming to pick up his clean clothes. When he came, I was brought to him and he would ask me how I was, but it was a formality; he would never touch me or look into my eyes. What was there to see in my eyes? Eunice washed, ironed, and folded his clothes; they were wrapped up like a gift in two pieces of clean nankeen cloth and placed on a table, the only table in the house, waiting for him to come and pick them up. His visits were quite regular, and so when he did not appear as he usually did, I noticed it. I said, "Where is my father?"

I said it in English—not French patois or English patois, but plain English—and that should have been the surprise: not that I spoke, but that I spoke English, a language I had never heard anyone speak. Ma Eunice and her children spoke the language of Dominica, which is French patois, and my father when he spoke to me spoke that language also, not because he disrespected me, but because he thought I understood nothing else. But no one noticed; they only marveled at the fact that I had finally spoken and inquired about the absence of my father. That the first words I said were in the language of a people I would never like or love is not now a mystery to me; everything in my life, good or bad, to which I am inextricably bound is a source of pain.

I was then four years old and saw the world as a series of soft lines joined together, a sketch in charcoal; and so when my father would come and take his clothes away I saw only that he suddenly appeared on the small path that led from the main road to the door of the house in which I lived and then, after completing his mission, disappeared as he turned onto the road where it met the path. I did not know what lay beyond the path, I did not know if after he passed from my sight he remained my father or dissolved into something altogether different and I would never see him again in the form of my father. I would have accepted this. I would have come to believe that this is the way of the world. I did not talk and I would not talk.

One day, without meaning to, I broke a plate, the only plate of its kind that Eunice had ever owned, a plate made of bone china, and the words "I am sorry" would not pass my lips. The sadness she expressed over this loss fascinated me; it was so thick with grief, so overwhelming, so deep, as if the death of a loved one had occurred. She grabbed the thick pouch that was her stomach, she pulled at her hair, she pounded her bosom; large tears rolled out of her eyes and down her cheeks, and they came in such profusion that if a new source of water had sprung up from them, as in a myth or a fairy tale, my small self would not have been surprised. I had been warned repeatedly by her not to touch this plate, for she had seen me look at it with an obsessive curiosity. I would look at it and wonder about the picture painted on its surface, a picture of a wide-open field filled with grass and flowers in the most tender shades of yellow, pink, blue, and green; the sky had a sun in it that shone but did not burn bright; the clouds were thin and scattered about like a decoration, not thick and banked up, not harbingers of doom. This picture was nothing but a field full of grass and flowers on a sunny day, but it had an atmosphere of secret abundance, happiness, and tranquillity; underneath it was written in gold letters the one word HEAVEN. Of course it was not a picture of heaven at all; it was a picture of the English countryside idealized, but I did not know that, I did not know that such a thing as the English countryside existed. And neither did Eunice; she thought that this picture was a picture of heaven, offering as it did a secret promise of a life without worry or care or want.

When I broke the china plate on which this picture was painted and caused Ma Eunice to cry so, I did not immediately feel sorry, I did not feel sorry shortly after, I felt sorry only long afterward, and by then it was too late to tell her so, she had died; perhaps she went to heaven and it fulfilled the promise on that plate. When I broke the plate and would not say that I was sorry, she cursed my dead mother, she cursed my father, she cursed me. The words she used were without meaning; I understood them but they did not hurt me, for I did not love her. And she did not love me. She made me kneel down on her stone heap, which as it should be was situated in a spot that got direct sun all day long, with my hands raised high above my head and with a large stone in each hand. She meant to keep me in this position until I said the words "I am sorry," but I would not say them, I could not say them. It was beyond my own will; those words could not pass my lips. I stayed like that until she exhausted herself cursing me and all whom I came from.

Why should this punishment have made a lasting impression on me, redolent as it was in every way of the relationship between captor and captive, master and slave, with its motif of the big and the small, the powerful and the powerless, the strong and the weak, and against a background of earth, sea, and sky, and Eunice standing over me, metamorphosing into a succession of things furious and not human with each syllable that passed her lips —with her dress of a thin, badly woven cotton, the bodice of a color and pattern contrary to the skirt, her hair, uncombed, unwashed for many months, wrapped in a piece of old cloth that had been unwashed for longer than her hair? The dress again —it had once been new and clean, and dirt had made it old, but dirt had made it new again by giving it shadings it did not have before, and dirt would finally cause it to disintegrate altogether, though she was not a dirty woman, she washed her feet every night.

The day was clear, it was not the rainy time, some men were on the sea casting nets for fish, but they would not catch too many because it was a clear day; and three of her children were eating bread and they rolled up the inside of the bread into small pebble-like shapes and threw them at me as I knelt there, and laughed at me; and the sky was without a cloud and there was not a breeze; a fly flew back and forth across my face, sometimes landing on a corner of my mouth; an overripe breadfruit fell off its tree, and that sound was like a fist meeting the soft, fleshy part of a body. All this, all this I can remember—why should it have made a lasting impression on me?

As I was kneeling there I saw three land turtles crawling in and out of the small space under the house, and I fell in love with them, I wanted to have them near me, I wanted to speak only to them each day for the rest of my life. Long after my ordeal was over—resolved in a way that did not please Ma Eunice, for I did not say I was sorry—I took all three turtles and placed them in an enclosed area where they could not come and go as they pleased and so were completely dependent on me for their existence. I would bring to them the leaves of vegetables and water in small seashells. I thought them beautiful, their shells dark gray with faint yellow circles, their long necks, their unjudging eyes, the slow deliberateness of their crawl. But they would withdraw into their shells when I did not want them to, and when I called them, they would not come out. To teach them a lesson, I took some mud from the riverbed and covered up the small hole from which each neck would emerge, and I allowed it to dry up. I covered over the place where they lived with stones, and for many days afterward I forgot about them. When they came into my mind again, I went to take a look at them in the place where I had left them. They were by then all dead.

It was my father's wish that I be sent to school. It was an unusual request; girls did not attend school, none of Ma Eunice's girl children attended school. I shall never know what made him do such a thing. I can only imagine that he desired such a thing for me without giving it too much thought, because in the end what could an education do for someone like me? I can only say what I did not have; I can only measure it against what I did have and find misery in the difference. And yet, and yet . . . it was for this reason that I came to see for the first time what lay beyond the path that led away from my house. And I can so well remember the feel of the cloth of my skirt and blouse—coarse because it was new—a green skirt and beige blouse, a uniform, its colors and style mimicking the colors and style of a school somewhere else, somewhere far away; and I had on a pair of brown thick cloth shoes and brown cotton socks which my father had gotten for me, I did not know where. And to mention that I did not know where these things came from, to say that I wondered about them, is really to say that this was the first time I had worn such things as shoes and socks, and they caused my feet to ache and swell and the skin to blister and break, but I was made to wear them until my feet got used to them, and my feet—all of me—did. That morning was a morning like any other, so ordinary it was profound: it was sunny in some places and not in others, and the two (sunny, cloudy) occupied different parts of the sky quite comfortably; there was the green of the leaves, the red burst of the flowers from the flamboyant trees, the sickly yellow fruit of the cashew, the smell of lime, the smell of almonds, the coffee on my breath, Eunice's skirt blowing in my face, and the stirring up of the smells that came from between her legs, which I shall never forget, and whenever I smell myself I am reminded of her. The river was low, so I did not hear the sound of the water rushing over stones; the breeze was soft, so the leaves did not rustle in the trees.

I had these sensations of seeing, smelling, and hearing on my journey down the path on the way to my school. When I reached the road and placed my newly shod feet on it, this was the first time I had done so. I was aware of this. It was a road of small stones and tightly packed dirt, and each step I took was awkward; the ground shifted, my feet slipped backward. The road stretched out ahead of me and vanished around a bend; we kept walking toward this bend and then we came to the bend and the bend gave way to more of the same road and then another bend. We came to my school before the end of the last bend. It was a small building with one door and four windows; it had a wooden floor; there was a small reptile crawling along a beam in the roof; there were three long desks lined up one behind the other; there was a large wooden table and a chair facing the three long desks; on the wall behind the wooden table and chair was a map; at the top of the map were the words "THE BRITISH EMPIRE." These were the first words I learned to read.

In that room always there were only boys; I did not sit in a schoolroom with other girls until I was older. I was not afraid in that new situation: I did not know how to be that then and do not know how to be that now. I was not afraid, because my mother had already died and that is the only thing a child is really afraid of; when I was born, my mother was dead, and I had already lived all those years with Eunice, a woman who was not my mother and who could not love me, and without my father, never knowing when I would see him again, so I was not afraid for myself in this situation. (And if it is not really true that I was not afraid then, it was not the only time that I did not admit to myself my own vulnerability.)

If I speak now of those first days with clarity and insight, it is not an invention, it should not surprise; at the time, each thing as it took place stood out in my mind with a sharpness that I now take for granted; it did not then have a meaning, it did not have a context, I did not yet know the history of events, I did not know their antecedents. My teacher was a woman who had been trained by Methodist missionaries; she was of the African people, that I could see, and she found in this a source of humiliation and self-loathing, and she wore despair like an article of clothing, like a mantle, or a staff on which she leaned constantly, a birthright which she would pass on to us. She did not love us; we did not love her; we did not love one another, not then, not ever. There were seven boys and myself. The boys, too, were all of the African people. My teacher and these boys looked at me and looked at me: I had thick eyebrows; my hair was coarse, thick, and wavy; my eyes were set far apart from each other and they had the shape of almonds; my lips were wide and narrow in an unexpected way. I was of the African people, but not exclusively. My mother was a Carib woman, and when they looked at me this is what they saw: The Carib people had been defeated and then exterminated, thrown away like the weeds in a garden; the African people had been defeated but had survived. When they looked at me, they saw only the Carib people. They were wrong but I did not tell them so.

I started to speak quite openly then—to myself frequently, to others only when it was absolutely necessary. We spoke English in school—proper English, not patois—and among ourselves we spoke French patois, a language that was not considered proper at all, a language that a person from France could not speak and could only with difficulty understand. I spoke to myself because I grew to like the sound of my own voice. It had a sweetness to me, it made my loneliness less, for I was lonely and wished to see people in whose faces I could recognize something of myself. Because who was I? My mother was dead; I had not seen my father for a long time.

I learned to read and write very quickly. My memory, my ability to retain information, to retrieve the tiniest detail, to recall who said what and when, was regarded as unusual, so unusual that my teacher, who was trained to think only of good and evil and whose judgment of such things was always mistaken, said I was evil, I was possessed—and to establish that there could be no doubt of this, she pointed again to the fact that my mother was of the Carib people.

My world then—silent, soft, and vegetable-like in its vulnerability, subject to the powerful whims of others, diurnal, beginning with the pale opening of light on the horizon each morning and ending with the sudden onset of dark at the beginning of each night—was both a mystery to me and the source of much pleasure: I loved the face of a gray sky, porous, grainy, wet, following me to school for mornings on end, sending down on me soft arrows of water; the face of that same sky when it was a hard, unsheltering blue, a backdrop for a cruel sun; the harsh heat that eventually became a part of me, like my blood; the overbearing trees (the stems of some of them the size of small trunks) that grew without restraint, as if beauty were only size, and I could tell them all apart by closing my eyes and listening to the sound the leaves made when they rubbed together; and I loved that moment when the white flowers from the cedar tree started to fall to the ground with a silence that I could hear, their petals at first still fresh, a soft kiss of pink and white, then a day later, crushed, wilted, and brown, a nuisance to the eye; and the river that had become a small lagoon when one day on its own it changed course, on whose bank I would sit and watch families of birds, and frogs laying their eggs, and the sky turning from black to blue and blue to black, and rain falling on the sea beyond the lagoon but not on the mountain that was beyond the sea. It was while sitting in this place that I first began to dream about my mother; I had fallen asleep on the stones that covered the ground around me, my small body sinking into this surface as if it were feathers. I saw my mother come down a ladder. She wore a long white gown, the hem of it falling just above her heels, and that was all of her that was exposed, just her heels; she came down and down, but no more of her was ever revealed. Only her heels, and the hem of her gown. At first I longed to see more, and then I became satisfied just to see her heels coming down toward me. When I awoke, I was not the same child I had been before I fell asleep. I longed to see my father and to be in his presence constantly.

On a day that began in no special way that I can remember, I was taught the principles involved in writing an ordinary letter. A letter has six parts: the address of the sender, the date, the address of the recipient, the salutation or greeting, the body of the letter, the closing of the letter. It was well known that a person in the position that I was expected to occupy—the position of a woman and a poor one—would have no need whatsoever to write a letter, but the sense of satisfaction it gave everyone connected with teaching me this, writing a letter, must have been immense. I was beaten and harsh words were said to me when I made a mistake. The exercise of copying the letters of someone whose complaints or perceptions or joys were of no interest to me did not make me angry then—I was too young to understand that vanity could be a weapon as dangerous as any knife; it only made me want to write my own letters, letters in which I would express my feelings about my own life as it appeared to me at seven years old. I started to write to my father. I wrote, "My dear Papa," in a lovely, decorative penmanship, a penmanship born of beatings and harsh words. I would say to him that I was mistreated by Eunice in word and deed and that I missed him and loved him very much. I wrote the same thing over and over again. It was without detail. It was nothing but the plaintive cry of a small wounded animal: "My dear Papa, you are the only person I have left in the world, no one loves me, only you can, I am beaten with words, I am beaten with sticks, I am beaten with stones, I love you more than anything, only you can save me." These words were not meant for my father at all but for the person of whom I could see only her heels. Night after night I saw her heels, only her heels coming down to meet me, coming down to meet me forever.

I wrote these letters without any intention of

sending them to my father; I did not know how to do that, to send them. I folded them up in such a way that if they were torn apart they would make eight small squares. There was no mysterious significance to this; I did it only to make them fit more discreetly under a large stone just outside the gate to my school. Each day, as I left, I would place a letter I had written to my father under it. I had written these letters in secret, during the small amount of time allotted to us as recess, or during the time when I had completed my work and had gone unnoticed. Pretending to be deeply involved in what I was supposed to be doing, I would write a letter to my father.

This small cry for help did not bring me instant relief. I recognized my own misery, but that it could be alleviated—that my life could change, that my circumstances could change—did not occur to me.

My letters did not remain a secret. A boy named Roman had seen me putting them in their secret place, and behind my back, he removed them. He had no empathy, no pity; any instinct to protect the weak had been destroyed in him. He took my letters to our teacher. In my letters to my father I had said, "Everyone hates me, only you love me," but I had not truly meant these letters to be sent to my father, and they were not really addressed to my father; if I had been asked then if I really felt that everyone hated me, that only my father loved me, I would not have known how to answer. But my teacher's reaction to my letters, those small scribblings, was a tonic to me. She believed the "everybody" I referred to was herself, and only herself. She said my words were a lie, libelous, that she was ashamed of me, that she was not afraid of me. My teacher said all this to me in front of the other pupils at my school. They thought I was humiliated and they felt joy seeing me brought so low. I did not feel humiliated at all. I felt something. I could see her teeth were crooked and yellow, and I wondered how they had got that way. Large half-moons of perspiration stained the underarms of her dress, and I wondered if when I became a woman I, too, would perspire so profusely and how it would smell. Behind her shoulder on the wall was a large female spider carrying its sac of eggs, and I wanted to reach out and crush it with the bare palm of my hand, because I wondered if it was the same kind of spider or a relative of the spider that had sucked saliva from the corner of my mouth the night before as I lay sleeping, leaving three small, painful bites. There was a drizzle of rain outside, I could hear the sound of it on the galvanized roof.

She sent my letters to my father, to show me that she had a clear conscience. She said that I had mistaken her scoldings, which were administered out of love for me, as an expression of hatred, and that this showed I was guilty of the sin of pride. And she said that she hoped I would learn to tell the difference between the two: love and hate. To this day, I have tried to tell the difference between the two, and I cannot, because often they wear so much the same face. When she said this, I did look in her face to see if I could tell whether it was true that she loved me and to see if her words, which so often seemed to be a series of harsh blows, were really an expression of love. Her face to me then did not appear loving, but perhaps I was mistaken—perhaps I was too young to judge, too young to know.

I did not immediately recognize what had happened, what I had done: however unconsciously, however without direction, I had, through the use of some words, changed my situation; I had perhaps even saved my life. To speak of my own situation, to myself or to others, is something I would always do thereafter. It is in this way that I came to be so extremely conscious of myself, so interested in my own needs, so interested in fulfilling them, aware of my grievances, aware of my pleasures. From this unfocused, childish expression of pain, my life was changed and I took note of it.

My father came to fetch me wearing the uniform of a jailer. To him this had no meaning, it was without significance. He was returning to Roseau from the village of St. Joseph, where he had been carrying out his duties as a policeman. I was not told that he would arrive on that day; I had not expected him. I returned from school and saw him standing at the final bend in the road that led to the house in which I lived. I was surprised to see him, but I would admit this only to myself; I did not let anyone know. The reason I had missed my father so—the reason he no longer came to the house in which I lived, bringing his dirty clothes and taking away clean ones—was that he had married again. I had been told about this, but it was a mystery to me what it might mean; it was not unlike the first time I had been told that the world was round; I thought, What can it mean, why should it be? My father had married again. He took my hand, he said something, he spoke in English, his mouth began to curl around the words he spoke, and it made him appear benign, attractive, even kind. I understood what he said: He had a home for me now, a good home; I would love his wife, my new mother; he loved me as much as he loved himself, perhaps even more, because I reminded him of someone whom he knew with certainty he had loved even more than he had loved himself. I would love my new home; I would love the sky above me and the earth below.

The word "love" was spoken with such frequency that it became a clue to my seven-year-old heart and my seven-year-old mind that this thing did not exist. My father's eyes grew small and then they grew big; he believed what he said, and that was a good thing, because I did not. But I would not have wanted to stop this progression, this new thing, this going away from here; and I did not believe him, but I did not have any reason to, no real reason. I was not yet cynical and thought that behind everything I heard lay another story altogether, the real story.

I thanked Eunice for taking care of me. I did not mean it, I could not mean it, I did not know how to mean it, but I would mean it now. I did not say goodbye; in the world that I lived in then and the world that I live in now, goodbyes do not exist, it is a small world. All my belongings were in a muslin knapsack and he placed them in a bag that was on the donkey he had been riding. He placed me on the donkey and sat behind me. And this was how we looked as my back was turned on the small house in which I spent the first seven years of my life: an already important man and his small daughter on the back of a donkey at the end of the day, an ordinary day, a day that had no meaning if you were less than a smudge on a page covered with print. I could hear my father's breath; it was not the breath of my life. The back of my head touched his chest from time to time, I could hear the sound of his heart beating through his shirt, the uniform that, when people saw him wearing it coming toward them, made them afraid, for his presence when wearing these clothes was almost always not a good thing. In my life then his presence was a good thing, it was too bad that he had not thought of changing his clothes; it was too bad that I had noticed he had not done so, it was too bad that such a thing would matter to me.

This new experience of really leaving the past behind, of going from one place to the other and knowing that whatever had been would remain just so, was something I immediately accepted as a gift, as a right of nature. This most simple of movements, the turning of your back, is among the most difficult to make, but once it has been made you cannot imagine it was at all hard to accomplish. I had not been able to do it by myself, but I could see that I had set in motion events that would make it possible. If I were ever to find myself sitting in that schoolroom again, or sitting in Eunice's yard again, sleeping in her bed, eating with her children, none of it would have the same power it once had over me—the power to make me feel helpless and ashamed at my own helplessness.

I could not see the look on my father's face as he rode, I did not know what he was thinking, I did not know him well enough to guess. He set off down the road in the opposite direction from the schoolhouse. The stretch of road was new to me, and yet it had a familiarity that made me sad. Around each bend was the familiar dark green of the trees that grew with a ferociousness that no hand had yet attempted to restrain, a green so unrelenting that it attained great beauty and great ugliness and yet great humility all at once; it was itself: nothing could be added to it; nothing could be taken away from it. Each precipice along the road was steep and dangerous, and a fall down one of them would have resulted in death or a lasting injury. And each climb up was followed by a slope down, at the bottom of which was the same choke of flowering plants, each with a purpose not yet known to me. And each curve that ran left would soon give way to a curve that ran right.

The day then began to have the colors of an ending, the colors of a funeral, gray, mauve, black; my sadness inside became manifest to me. I was a part of a procession of sadness, which was moving away from my old life, a life I had lived for only seven years. I did not become overwhelmed, though. The dark of night came on with its usual suddenness, without warning. Again I did not become overwhelmed. My father placed an arm around me, as if to ward off something—a danger I could not see in the cool air, an evil spirit, a fall. His clasp was at first gentle; then it grew till it had the strength of an iron band, but even then I did not become overwhelmed.

We entered the village in the dark. There were no lights anywhere, no dog barked, we did not pass anyone. We entered the house in which my father lived, there was a light coming from a beautiful glass lamp, something I had never seen before; the light was fueled by a clear liquid that I could see through the base of the lamp, which was embossed with the heads of animals unfamiliar to me. The lamp was on a shelf, and the shelf was made of mahogany, its brackets ended in the shape of two tightly closed paws. The room was crowded, with a chair on which two people could sit at once, two other chairs on which only one person could sit, and a small, low table draped with a piece of white linen. The walls of the house and the partition that separated this room from the rest of the house were covered with paper, and the paper was decorated with small pink roses. I had never seen anything like this before, except once, while looking through a book at my school—but the picture I had seen then was a drawing illustrating a story about the domestic goings-on of a small mammal who lived in a field with his family. In their burrow, the walls had been covered with similar paper. I had understood that story about the small mammal to be a pretense, something to amuse a child, but this was my very real father's house, a house with a bright lamp in a room, and a room that seemed to exist only for an occasional purpose.

At that moment I realized that there were so many things I did not know, not including the very big thing I did not know—my mother. I did not know my father; I did not know where he was from or whom or what he liked; I did not know the land whose surface I had just come through on an animal's back; I did not know who I was or why I was standing there in that room of the occasional purpose with the lamp. A great sea of what I did not know opened up before me, and its powerful treacherous currents pulsed over my head repeatedly until I was sure I was dead.

I had only fainted. I opened my eyes soon after to see the face of my father's wife not too far above mine. She had the face of evil. I had no other face to compare it with; I knew only that hers was the face of evil as far as I could tell. She did not like me. I could see that. She did not love me. I could see that. I could not see the rest of her right away —only her face. She was of the African people and the people from France. It was nighttime and she was in her own house, so her hair was exposed; it was smooth and yet tightly curled, and she wore it parted in the middle and plaited in two braids that were pinned up in the back. Her lips were shaped like those of people from a cold climate: thin and ungenerous. Her eyes were black, not with beauty but with deceit. Her nose was long and sharp, like an arrow; her cheekbones were also sharp. She did not like me. She did not love me. I could see it in her face. My spirit rose to meet this challenge. No love: I could live in a place like this. I knew this atmosphere all too well. Love would have defeated me. Love would always defeat me. In an atmosphere of no love I could live well; in this atmosphere of no love I could make a life for myself. She held a cup to my mouth, one of her hands brushed against my face, and it felt cold; she was feeding me a tea, something to revive me, but it tasted bitter, like a bad potion. My small tongue allowed no more than a drop of it to come into my mouth, but the bitter taste of it warmed my young heart. I sat up. Our eyes did not meet and lock; I was too young to throw out such a challenge, I could then act only on instinct.

I was led down a short hallway to a room. It was to be my own room; my father lived in a house in which there were enough rooms for me to occupy my own. This small event immediately became central to my life: I adjusted to this evidence of privacy without question. My room was lit by a small lamp, the size of my now large, aged fist, and I could see my bed: small, of wood, a white sheet on its copra-filled mattress, a square, flat pillow. I had a wash-stand on which stood a basin and an urn that had water in it. I did not see a towel. (I did not then know how to wash myself properly, in any case, and the lesson I eventually got came with many words of abuse.) There was not a picture on the wall. The walls were not covered with paper; the bare wood, pine, was not painted. It was the plainest of plain rooms, but it had in it more luxury than I had ever imagined, it offered me something I did not even know I needed: it offered me solitude. All of my little being, physical and spiritual, could find peace here, in this little place of my own where I could sit and take stock.

I sat down on the bed. My heart was breaking; I wanted to cry, I felt so alone. I felt in danger, I felt threatened; I felt as each minute passed that someone wished me dead. My father's wife came to say good night, and she turned out the lamp. She spoke to me then in French patois; in his presence she had spoken to me in English. She would do this to me through all the time we knew each other, but that first time, in the sanctuary of my room, at seven years old, I recognized this to be an attempt on her part to make an illegitimate of me, to associate me with the made-up language of people regarded as not real—the shadow people, the forever humiliated, the forever low. She then went to the part of the house where she and my father slept; it was far enough away that I could hear the sound of her footsteps fade; still, I could hear their voices as they spoke, the sounds swirling upward to the empty space beneath the ceiling. They had a conversation; I could not make out the words; the emotions seemed neutral, neither hot nor cold. There was some silence; there were short gasps and sighs; there were the sounds of people sleeping, breath escaping through the mouth.

I lay down to sleep and to dream of my mother—for I knew I would do that, I knew I would make myself do that, I needed to do that. She came down the ladder again and again, over and over, just her heels and the hem of her white dress visible; down, down, over and over. I watched her all night in my dream. I did not see her face. I was not disappointed. I would have loved to see her face, but I didn't long for it anymore. She sang a song, but it had no words; it was not a lullaby, it was not sentimental, not meant to calm me when my soul roiled at the harshness of life; it was only a song, but the sound of her voice was like a small treasure found in an abandoned chest, a treasure that inspires not astonishment but contentment and eternal pleasure.

All night I slept, and in my sleep saw her feet

come down the ladder, step after step, never seeing her face, hearing her voice sing that song, sometimes humming, sometimes through an open mouth. To this day she will appear in my dreams from time to time but never again to sing or utter a sound of any kind—only as before, coming down a ladder, her heels visible and the white hem of her garment above them.

I came to my father's house in the blanket of voluptuous blackness that was the night; a morning naturally followed. I awoke in the false paradise into which I was born, the false paradise in which I will die, the same landscape that I had always known, each aspect of it beyond reproach, at once beautiful, ugly, humble, and proud; full of life, full of death, able to sustain the one, inevitably to claim the other.

My father's wife showed me how to wash myself. It was not done with kindness. My human form and odor were an opportunity to heap scorn on me. I responded in a fashion by now characteristic of me: whatever I was told to hate I loved and loved the most. I loved the smell of the thin dirt behind my ears, the smell of my unwashed mouth, the smell that came from between my legs, the smell in the pit of my arm, the smell of my unwashed feet. Whatever about me caused offense, whatever was native to me, whatever I could not help and was not a moral failing—those things about me I loved with the fervor of the devoted. Her hands as they touched me were cold and caused me pain. We would never love each other. In her was a despair rooted in a desire long thwarted: she had not yet been able to bear my father a child. She was afraid of me; she was afraid that because of me my father would think of my mother more often than he thought of her. On that first morning she gave me some food and it was old, moldy, as if she had saved it specially for me in order to make me sick. I did not eat what she gave me after that; I learned then how to prepare my own food and made this a trait by which others would know me: I was a girl who prepared her own food.

Parts of my life, incidents in my life then, seem, when I remember them now, as if they were happening in a very small, dark place, a place the size of a dollhouse, and the dollhouse is at the bottom of a hole, and I am way up at the top of the hole, peering down into this little house, trying to make out exactly what it is that happened down there. And sometimes when I look down at this scene, certain things are not in the same place they were in the last time I looked: different things are in the shadows at different times, different things are in the light.

My father's wife wished me dead, at first in a way that would have allowed her to make a lavish display of sorrow over my death: an accident, God's desire. And then when no accident occurred and God did not seem to care one way or the other whether I lived or died, she tried to accomplish this herself. She made me a present of a necklace fashioned from dried berries and polished wood and stone and shells from the sea. It was most beautiful, too beautiful for a child, but a child, a real child, would have been dazzled by it, would have been seduced by it, would have immediately placed it around her neck. I was not a real child. I thanked and thanked her. I thanked her again. I did not take it into my small room. I did not want to hold on to it for very long. I had made a small place in the everlastingly thick grove of trees at the back of the house. She did not know of it yet; when eventually she discovered it, she sent something that I could not see to live there and it drove me away. It was in this secret place that I left the necklace until I could decide what to do with it. She would look at my neck and notice that I was not wearing it, but she never mentioned it again. Not once. She never urged me to wear it at all. She had a dog that she took to ground with her; this dog was a gift from my father, it was to protect her from real human harm, a harm that could be seen, it was meant to make her feel a kind of safety. One day I placed the necklace around the dog's neck, hiding it in the hair there; within twenty-four hours he went mad and died. If she found the necklace around his neck she never mentioned it to me. She became pregnant then and bore the first of her two children, and this took her close attention away from me; but she did not stop wishing me dead.

The school I attended was five miles away in the next village, and I walked to it with some other children, most of them boys. We had to cross a river, but in the dry season that meant stepping on the stones in the riverbed. When it rained and the water had risen very high, we would remove our clothes and tie them in a bundle, placing them on our heads, and cross the river naked. One day when the river was very high and we were crossing naked, we saw a woman in the part of the river where the mouth met the sea. It was deep there and we could not tell if she was sitting or standing, but we knew she was naked. She was a beautiful woman, more beautiful than any woman we had ever seen, beautiful in a way that made sense to us, not a European way: she was dark brown in skin, her hair was black and shiny and twisted into small coils all around her head. Her face was like a moon, a soft, brown, glistening moon. She opened her mouth and a strange yet sweet sound came out. It was mesmerizing; we stood and stared at her. She was surrounded by fruit, mangoes—it was the season for them—and they were all ripe, and those shades of red, pink, and yellow were tantalizing and mouth-watering. She beckoned to us to come to her. Someone said it was not a woman at all, that we should not go, that we should run away. We could not move away. And then this boy, whose face I can remember because it was the male mask of heedlessness and boastfulness that I have come to know, started forward and forward, and he laughed as he went forward. When he seemed to get to the place where she was, she moved farther away, yet she was always in the same place; he swam toward her and the fruit, and each time he was almost near, she became farther away. He swam in this way until he began to sink from exhaustion; we could see only the top of his head, we could see only his hands; then we could see nothing at all, only a set of expanding circles where he used to be, as if a pebble had been thrown there. And then the woman with her fruit vanished, too, as if she had not been there, as if the whole thing had never happened.

The boy disappeared; he was never seen again, not dead even, and when the water got low in that place, we would go and look, but he wasn't there. It was as if it had never happened, and the way we talked about it was as if we had imagined it, because we never spoke about it out loud, we only accepted that it had happened, and it came to exist only in our minds, an act of faith, like the Virgin Birth for some people, or other such miracles; and it had the same power of belief and disbelief, only unlike the Virgin Birth we had seen this ourselves. I saw it happen. I saw a boy in whose company I would walk to school swim out naked to meet a woman who was also naked and surrounded by ripe fruit and disappear in the muddy waters where the river met the sea. He disappeared there and was never seen again. That woman was not a woman; she was a something that took the shape of a woman. It was almost as if the reality of this terror was so overwhelming that it became a myth, as if it had happened a very long time ago and to other people, not us. I know of friends who witnessed this event with me and, forgetting that I was present, would tell it to me in a certain way, daring me to believe them; but it is only because they do not themselves believe what they are saying; they no longer believe what they saw with their own eyes, or in their own reality. This is no longer without an explanation to me. Everything about us is held in doubt and we the defeated define all that is unreal, all that is not human, all that is without love, all that is without mercy. Our experience cannot be interpreted by us; we do not know the truth of it. Our God was not the correct one, our understanding of heaven and hell was not a respectable one. Belief in that apparition of a naked woman with outstretched arms beckoning a small boy to his death was the belief of the illegitimate, the poor, the low. I believed in that apparition then and I believe in it now.

Who was my father? Not just who was he to me, his child—but who was he? He was a policeman, but not an ordinary policeman; he inspired more than the expected amount of fear for someone in his position. He made appointments to see people, men, at his house, the place where he lived with his family—this entity of which I was now a sort of member—and he would make these people wait for hours; at times he never showed up at all. They waited for him, sometimes sitting on a stone that was just inside the gate of the yard, sometimes pacing back and forth from inside the yard to outside the yard, causing the gate to creak, and this always made his wife cross, and she would complain to these people, speaking rudely to them, the rudeness way out of proportion to the annoyance of the creaky gate. They waited for him without complaint, falling asleep standing up, falling asleep as they sat on the ground, flies drinking from the saliva that leaked out of the corners of their open mouths. They waited, and when he did not show up they left and returned the next day, hoping to see him; sometimes they did, sometimes they did not. He suffered no consequences for his behavior; he just treated people in this way. He did not care, or so I thought at first—but of course he did care; it was well thought out, this way he had of causing suffering; he was a part of a whole way of life on the island which perpetuated pain.

At the time I came to live with him, he had just mastered the mask that he wore as a face for the remainder of his life: the skin taut, the eyes small and drawn back as though deep inside his head, so that it wasn't possible to get a clue to him from them, the lips parted in a smile. He seemed trustworthy. His clothes were always well ironed, clean, spotless. He did not like people to know him very well; he tried never to eat food in the presence of strangers, or in the presence of people who were afraid of him.

Who was he? I ask myself this all the time, to this day. Who was he? He was a tall man; his hair was red; his eyes were gray. His wife, the woman he married after my mother died while giving birth to me, was the only daughter of a thief, a man who grew bananas and coffee and cocoa on his own land (these crops were sold to someone else, a European man who exported them). She came to my father with no money, but her father made possible many connections for him. They bought other people's land together, they divided the profits in a way satisfactory to them both, they never quarreled, but they did not seem to be close friends; my father did not have that, a close friend. When he met the daughter of his sometime partner in crime I do not know. It might have been a night full of stars, or a night with no light at all from above, or a day with the sun big in the sky or so bleak it felt sad to be alive. I do not know and I do not want to find out. Her voice had a harsh, heated quality to it; if there is a language that would make her voice sound musical and so invite desire, I do not yet know of it.

My father must have loved me then, but he never told me so. I never heard him say those words to anyone. He wanted me to keep going to school, he made sure of this, but I do not know why. He wanted me to go to school beyond the time that most girls were in school. I went to school past the age of thirteen. No one told me what I should do with myself after I was finished with school. It was a great sacrifice that I should go to school, because as his wife often pointed out, I would have been more useful at home. He gave me books to read. He gave me a life of John Wesley, and as I read it I wondered what the life of a man so full of spiritual tumult and piety had to do with me. My father had become a Methodist, he attended church every Sunday; he taught Sunday school. The more he robbed, the more money he had, the more he went to church; it is not an unheard-of linking. And the richer he became, the more fixed the mask of his face grew, so that now I no longer remember what he really looked like when I first knew him long ago, before I came to live with him. And so my mother and father then were a mystery to me: one through death, the other through the maze of living; one I had never seen, the other I saw constantly.

The world I came to know was full of danger and treachery, but I did not become afraid, I did not become cautious. I was not indifferent to the danger my father's wife posed to me, and I was not indifferent to the danger she thought my presence posed to her. So in my father's house, which was her home, I tried to cloak myself in an atmosphere of apology. I did not in fact feel sorry for anything at all, I had not done anything, either deliberately or by accident, that warranted my begging for forgiveness, but my gait was a weapon—a way of deflecting her attention from me, of persuading her to think of me as someone who was pitiable, an ignorant child. I did not like her, I did not wish her dead, I only wanted her to leave me alone. I was very careful how far I carried this attitude of piousness, because I did not wish to draw the sympathy of anyone else, especially not my father, for I calculated she might become jealous of that. I had a version of this piety that I took with me to school. To my teachers I seemed quiet and studious; I was modest, which is to say, I did not seem to them to have any interest in the world of my body or anyone else's body. This wearying demand was only one of many demands made on me simply because I was female. From the moment I stepped out of my bed in the early morning to the time I covered myself up again in the dark of night, I negotiated many treacherous acts of deception, but it was clear to me who I really was.

I lay in my bed at night, and turned my ear to the sounds that were inside and outside the house, identifying each noise, separating the real from the unreal: whether the screeches that crisscrossed the night, leaving the blackness to fall to earth like so many ribbons, were the screeches of bats or someone who had taken the shape of a bat; whether the sound of wings beating in that space so empty of light was a bird or someone who had taken the shape of a bird. The sound of the gate being opened was my father coming home long after the stillness of sleep had overtaken most of his household, his footsteps stealthy but sure, coming into the yard, up the steps; his hand opening the door to his house, closing the door behind him, turning the bar that made the door secure, walking to another part of the house; he never ate meals when he returned home late at night. The sound of the sea then, at night, could be heard so clearly, sometimes as a soft swish, a lapping of waves against the shore of black stones, sometimes with the anger of water boiling in a cauldron resting unsteadily on a large fire. And sometimes when the night was completely still and completely black, I could hear, outside, the long sigh of someone on the way to eternity; and this, of all things, would disturb the troubled peace of all that was real: the dogs asleep under houses, the chickens in the trees, the trees themselves moving about, not in a way that suggested an uprooting, just a moving about, as if they wished they could run away. And if I listened again I could hear the sound of those who crawled on their bellies, the ones who carried poisonous lances, and those who carried a deadly poison in their saliva; I could hear the ones who were hunting, the ones who were hunted, the pitiful cry of the small ones who were about to be devoured, followed by the temporary satisfaction of the ones doing the devouring: all this I heard night after night, again and again. And it ended only after my hands had traveled up and down all over my own body in a loving caress, finally coming to the soft, moist spot between my legs, and a gasp of pleasure had escaped my lips which I would allow no one to hear.

It perhaps was inevitable that as soon as I came to know the long walk from my father's house to my school in the next village like the back of my hand, I was to leave it behind. This walk, all five miles of it one way, five miles of it the other, never ceased to be of some terror for all the children who walked it, and we tried never to be alone. We walked in groups always. In any one year, at any one time, there were not more than a dozen of us, more boys than girls. We were not friends; such a thing was discouraged. We were never to trust each other. This was like a motto repeated to us by our parents; it was a part of my upbringing, like a form of good manners: You cannot trust these people, my father would say to me, the very words the other children's parents were saying to them, perhaps even at the same time. That "these people" were ourselves, that this insistence on mistrust of others—that people who looked so very much like each other, who shared a common history of suffering and humiliation and enslavement, should be taught to mistrust each other, even as children, is no longer a mystery to me. The people we should naturally have mistrusted were beyond our influence completely; what we needed to defeat them, to rid ourselves of them, was something far more powerful than mistrust. To mistrust each other was just one of the many feelings we had for each other, all of them the opposite of love, all of them standing in the place of love. It was as if we were in competition with each other for a secret prize, and we were afraid that someone else would get it; any expression of love, then, would not be sincere, for love might give someone else the advantage.

We were not friends. We walked together in a companionship based on fear, fear of things we could not see, and when those things were seen, we often could not really comprehend their danger, so confusing was much of reality. It was only after we had left the immediate confines of our village and were out of the sight of our parents that we drew close to each other. We would talk, but our conversation was always about terror. How could it not be so? We had seen that boy drown in the mouth of the river we crossed each day. If our schooling was successful, most of us would not have believed we had witnessed such a thing. To say that we had seen this boy float out to meet a woman surrounded by fruit, and then vanish in the swollen waters in the mouth of the river, was to say that we lived in a darkness from which we could not be redeemed. I then and now had and have no use for redemption.

My father did not believe that I had witnessed the boy's drowning. He was angry with me for saying I had seen it; he blamed the company I kept. He said I was not to speak to those other children; he said they did not come from good homes or good people; he said that I should remember that he was my father and that he occupied an important official position and that for me to say such things could only cause him embarrassment. I remember mostly the way he told me that I did not see what I knew, and still know: what I had seen. My father had inherited the ghostly paleness of his own father, the skin that looks as if it is waiting for another skin, a real skin, to come and cover it up, and his eyes were gray, like his own father's eyes, and his hair was a red and brown like his father's also; only the texture of his hair, thick and tightly curled, was like his mother's. She was a woman from Africa, where in Africa no one knew, and what good would it do to find out, she was simply from somewhere in Africa, that place on the map which was a configuration of shapes and shades of yellow. And he pointed his brownish-pink, pinkish-brown finger at me and said that I had not seen what I had seen, could not have seen what I had seen, did not, did not, did not; but I did, I did, I did. But it was not to him that I insisted on the reality I knew. And I did not tell him of the day when, returning from school alone, I saw a spotted monkey sitting in a tree and I threw three stones at it. The monkey caught the third one and threw it back at me and struck me over my left eye, in the hair of my brow, and I bled furiously, as if I would never stop. I somehow knew that the red berries of a certain bush would stop the flow of blood. My father, when he saw my wound, thought that it had come from the hands of a schoolmate, a boy, someone I was so protective of I would not reveal his identity. It was then that he began to make plans to send me to school in Roseau, to get me away from the bad influence of children who would wound me, whom I was protecting from his wrath, and who, he was certain, were male. And after this outburst of emotion, meant as an expression of his love for me but which only made me feel anew the hatred and isolation in which we all lived, his face again became a mask, impossible to read.

On that road which I came to know so well, I spent some of the sweetest moments of my life. On a long stretch of it in the late afternoon I could see the reflection of the sun's light on the surface of the seawater, and it always had the quality of an expectation just about to be fulfilled, as if at any moment a small city made out of that special light of the sun on the water would arise, and from it might flow a joy I had not yet imagined. And I knew a place just off the side of this road where the sweetest cashews grew; the juice from their fruit would cause blisters to form on my lips and make my tongue feel as if it were caught in a bundle of twine, temporarily making speech difficult, and I found this, the difficulty of speaking, the possibility that it might be a struggle for me ever to speak again, delicious. It was on that road that I first walked directly from one kind of weather system to another: from a cold, heavy rain to a bright, clear heat of midday. And it was on that road that my sister, the girl child of my father and his wife, was traveling on a bicycle after meeting a man my father had forbidden her to see and whom she would marry, when she had an accident, falling over a precipice, which left her lame and barren, her eyes unable to focus properly. This is not a happy memory; her suffering, even now, is very real to me.

Not long after I came to live with them, my father's wife began to have her own children. She bore a boy first, then she had a girl. This had two predictable outcomes: she left me alone and she valued her son more than her daughter. That she did not think very much of the person who was most like her, a daughter, a female, was so normal that it would have been noticed only if it had been otherwise: to people like us, despising anything that was most like ourselves was almost a law of nature. This fact of my sister's life made me feel overwhelmingly sympathetic to her. She did not like me—she was told by her mother that I was an enemy of hers, that I was not to be trusted, that I was like a thief in the house, waiting for the right moment when I would rob them of their inheritance. This was convincing to my sister, and she distrusted me and she disliked me; the first words of insult she could speak were directed toward me. My father's wife had always said to me, in private, when my father was not there, that I could not be his child because I did not look like him, and it was true that I did not have any of his physical characteristics. My sister, though, did look like him: her hair and eyes were the same color as his, red and gray; her skin, too, was the same color as his, thin and red, not the red of his hair, another red, like the color of the earth in some places. But she did not have his calm or his patience; she walked like a warrior and could not contain the fury that was inside her. Nor did she have his quality of keeping her own counsel; every thought that came into her mind had to be voiced, so that whenever she saw me, she would let me know immediately whatever my presence suggested to her. I never hated her, I had only sympathy for her. Her tragedy was greater than mine; her mother did not love her, but her mother was alive, and every day she saw her mother and every day her mother let her know she was not loved. My mother was dead. It was her own son that my father's wife favored, not loved more, for she was incapable of it—love; she favored him because he was not like her: he was not female, he was male. This boy thought, and was encouraged to think, that he was like his father in ways that were physical and in ways that were spiritual, so that it was said of him that he walked like his father and that certain of his gestures were like his father's, but it was not true; it was not so, not really. He did walk like my father, he did have some of his gestures, but this walk of my father's was not natural to my father and his gestures were not natural to him, either. My father had invented himself, had made himself up as he went along; when he wanted something, he made himself meet the situation, he made his cut fit the jib. The man, my father, whom his wife and his son saw, the man they wanted that boy to be, existed, but the person they saw was an expression of my father's desires, an expression of his needs; the personality they were observing was like a suit of clothes my father had made for himself, and eventually he wore it so long that it became impossible to remove, it covered completely who he really was; who he really might have been became unknown, even to himself. My father was a thief, he was a jailer, he spoke falsehoods, he took advantage of the weak; that was who was he was at heart; he acted in these ways at all times in his life, but by the end of his life, the jailer, the thief, the liar, the coward—all were unknown to him. He believed himself to be a man of freedom, honest and brave; he believed it as he believed in the realness of anything he could see standing in front of him, like the warmth of the sun or the blueness of the sky, and nothing could convince him that just the opposite was the truth. This was not something his wife and her son would have known, or could have known, and so this boy from his beginning lived a painful life, a copied life, a life whose origins he did not know. To see him, when he was eleven years old or so, wearing a white linen suit, a direct copy of his father's; so thin, so pale; his black hair, which was the same as his mother's, forced down straight against his scalp; his gait awkward, unsteady, as if he had only just mastered the ability to use his feet—to see him walking to church, to worship a god my father did not really believe in, because my father could not believe in any god; to see him try so very hard to be like this man he did not know, whose actions he had never examined, inspired in me only pity and sadness; and so when he died, before he was nineteen years of age, I did not feel it was a tragedy, I only felt it was merciful that his life of misery and torture should be so short. His death was long and painful, its cause unknown, perhaps even unknowable; when he died there was no empty space where he had been, and his mother's grief and my father's grief for him would often seem mysterious, a big why and what, because who was this boy, this person whom they grieved over.

And so I had come to know well the world in which I was living. I knew how to interpret the long silences my father's wife had constructed between us. Sometimes in these silences there was nothing at all; sometimes they were filled with pure evil; sometimes she meant to see me dead, sometimes my being alive was of no interest to her. Her wishing me dead was an automatic response; she had never loved me, she had never wished to see me alive in the first place, and so when she saw me, really saw me, looked at me and realized who I was, she could only wish me dead. But after her first real attempt —the one in which she made me a gift of a necklace, which I then presented as a gift to her favorite dog and the necklace gave the dog the death that was meant for me—the other attempts she made were only halfhearted; this was partly because she recognized my desire to survive and partly because she had become preoccupied with her life as the mother of a great man to be. When her son died, I was no longer living in her house, I had passed out of her view, she did not have me to look on and perhaps take revenge on because I went on living.

Observing any human being from infancy, seeing someone come into existence, like a new flower in bud, each petal first tightly furled around another, and then the natural loosening and unfurling, the opening into a bloom, the life of that bloom, must be something wonderful to behold; to see experience collect in the eyes, around the corners of the mouth, the weighing down of the brow, the heaviness in heart and soul, the thick gathering around the waist, the breasts, the slowing down of footsteps not from old age but only with the caution of life—all this is something so wonderful to observe, so wonderful to behold; the pleasure for the observer, the beholder, is an invisible current between the two, observed and observer, beheld and beholder, and I believe that no life is complete, no life is really whole, without this invisible current, which is in many ways a definition of love. No one observed and beheld me, I observed and beheld myself; the invisible current went out and it came back to me. I came to love myself in defiance, out of despair, because there was nothing else. Such a love will do, but it will only do, it is not the best kind; it has the taste of something left out on a shelf too long that has turned rancid, and when eaten makes the stomach turn. It will do, it will do, but only because there is nothing else to take its place; it is not to be recommended.

And so it was that when I first saw the thick red fluid of my menstrual blood, I was not surprised and not afraid. I had never heard of it, I had not been expecting it, I was twelve years old, but its appearance to my young mind, to my body and soul, had the force of destiny fulfilled; it was as if I had always known of it but had never admitted it to consciousness, had never known how to put it into words. It appeared that first time so thick and red and plentiful that it was impossible to think of it as only an omen, a warning of some kind, a symbol; it was just its real self, my menstrual flow, and I knew immediately that its failure to appear regularly after a certain interval could only mean a great deal of trouble for me. Perhaps I knew then that the child in me would never be stilled enough to allow me to have a child of my own. From a baker I bought four bags, the kind in which flour was shipped, and after removing the dyed brand markings through a long process of washing and bleaching in the hot sun, I made four squares from each and used them as napkins to catch my blood as it flowed from between my legs. After my father's wife saw me initiate and complete this one act, she said to me that when I became a real woman, she would have to guard herself against me. At the time I felt such a statement to be unwarranted, for after all I was still on my guard when it came to her. It was around then, too, that the texture of my body and the smell of my body began to change; coarse hairs appeared under my arms and in the space between my legs where there had been none, my hips widened, my chest thickened and swelled up slightly at first, and a deep space formed between my two breasts; the hair on my head grew long and soft and the waves in it deepened, my lips spread across my face and thickened into the shape of a heart that had been stepped on. I used to stare at myself in an old piece of a broken looking glass I had found in some rubbish under my father's house. The sight of my changing self did not frighten me, I only wondered how I would look eventually; I never doubted that I would like completely whatever stared back at me. And so, too, the smell of my underarms and between my legs changed, and this change pleased me. In those places the smell became pungent, sharp, as if something was in the process of fermenting, slowly; in private, then as now, my hands almost never left those places, and when I was in public, these same hands were always not far from my nose, I so enjoyed the way I smelled, then and now.

At the age of fourteen, I had exhausted the resources of the tiny school in Massacre, the tiny village between Roseau and Mahaut. I really knew much more than that school could teach me. I could sense from the beginning of my life that I would know things when I needed to know them, I had known a long time ago that I could trust my own instincts about things, that if I were ever in a difficult situation, if I thought about it long enough a solution would appear to me. That there would be limitations to having such a view of life I could not know, but in any case, my life was already small and limited in its own way.

I also knew the history of an array of people I would never meet. That in itself should not have kept me from knowing of them; it was only that this history of peoples that I would never meet—Romans, Gauls, Saxons, Britons, the British people—had behind it a malicious intent: to make me feel humiliated, humbled, small. Once I had identified and accepted this malice directed at me, I became fascinated with this expression of vanity: the perfume of your own name and your own deeds is intoxicating, and it never causes you to feel weary or exhausted; it is its own inspiration, it is its own renewal. And I learned, too, that no one can truly judge himself; to describe your own transgressions is to forgive yourself for them; to confess your bad deeds is also at once to forgive yourself, and so silence becomes the only form of self-punishment: to live forever locked up in an iron cage made of your own silence, and then, from time to time, to have this silence broken by a designated crier, someone who repeats over and over, in broken or complete sentences, a list of the violations, the bad deeds committed.

I had never been to Roseau until that day in my fifteenth year when my father took me to the house of a man he knew, Monsieur LaBatte, Monsieur Jacques LaBatte, Jack, as I came to call him in the bitter and sweet dark of night. He, too, was a man of no principles, and this did not surprise or disappoint me, this did not make me like him more or less. He and my father knew each other through financial arrangements they made with each other. They called each other friend, but the fragility of the foundation on which this friendship was built would cause only sadness in someone who does not love the world and all the material things in it. And Roseau, even then, when the reality of every situation was so horrible that it had to be disguised and called something else, something the opposite of its true self, was not referred to as a city, it was called the capital, the capital of Dominica. It, too, had a fragile foundation, and from time to time was destroyed by forces of nature, a hurricane or water coming from the sky as if suddenly the sea were above and the heavens below. Roseau could not be called a city, because it could not embody such noble aspirations—center of commerce and culture and exchange of ideas among people, place of intrigue, place in which plots are hatched and the destinies of many are determined; it was no such thing as a city, it was an outpost, a way station for people for whom things had gone wrong, either because of their own actions or through no fault of their own; and there were then many places like Roseau, outposts of despair; for conqueror and conquered alike these places were the capitals of nothing but despair. This did not surprise the ones forcibly brought to live in such a place, but even so, in this place there was some beauty, unexpected and therefore thrilling; it could be seen in the way the houses were all closely pressed together, jammed up, small and crooked, as if ill built on purpose, painted in the harsh hues of red, blue, green, or yellow, or sometimes not painted at all, the bare wood exposed to the elements, turning a bright gray. In this sort of house lived people whose skins glistened with exhaustion and whose faces were sad even when they had a reason to be happy, people for whom history had been a big, dark room, which made them hate silence. And sometimes there was a gentle wind and sometimes the stillness of the trees, and sometimes the sun setting and sometimes the dawn opening up, and the sweet, sickening smell of the white lily that bloomed only at night, and the sweet, sickening smell of something dead, something animal, rotting. This beauty, when I first saw it—I saw it in parts, not all at once—made me glad to be alive; I could not explain this feeling of gladness at the sight of the new and strange, the unfamiliar. And then long, long after, when all these things had become a part of me, a part of my every day, this feeling of gladness was no longer possible, but I would yearn for it, to feel new again, to feel within myself a fountain of joy springing up, to feel full of hope, to feel young again. I long now to feel fresh again, to feel I will never die, but that is not possible; I can only long for it, I can never be that way again.

Long after my father removed me from his house and the presence of his wife, I came to understand that he knew it was necessary to do so. I never knew what he noticed about me, I never knew what he wanted of me or from me; at the time it seemed to have a purpose, this removing me to Roseau; he wanted me to continue to go to school, he wanted me to someday become a schoolteacher, he wanted to say that his daughter was a teacher in a school. That I might have had aspirations of my own would not have occurred to him, and if I had aspirations of my own, I did not know of them. How the atmosphere in his own house felt to him I did not know. What he saw in my face he never told me. But he took me to this house of a man he knew in business and left me in the care of this man and his wife. I was a boarder, but I paid my own way. In exchange for my room and board in this house I performed some household tasks. I did not object, I could not object, I did not want to object, I did not know then how to object openly.

I met Monsieur and Madame in the afternoon, a hot afternoon. They were that to me then—Monsieur and Madame. I met her first, alone; he was in a room by himself, in another part of their house, a room where he kept money which he liked to count over and over again; it was not all the money in the world that he had. When I first met Madame LaBatte, she was standing in the doorway of her nice house, the front doorway, with its nice clean yard full of flowers and piles of stones neatly arranged; to her left and to her right were two large clumps of plumbago with blue flowers still in the hot air. She wore a white dress made of a coarse cloth decorated with embroidery stitching of flowers and leaves; I noticed this because it was a dress people in Mahaut would have worn only to church on Sundays. Her dress was not worn out and it was clean; it was not in a stylish cut but loose, fitting her badly, as if her body was no longer of any interest to her. My father spoke to her, she spoke to my father, she spoke to me; she looked at me, I looked at her. It was not to size each other up; I did not know what she thought she saw in my eyes, but I can say now that I had an instinctive feeling of sympathy for her. I did not know why sympathy, why not the opposite of that, but sympathy was what I felt all the same. It might have been because she looked so much like someone who had gotten something she so very much wanted.

She had very much wanted to marry Monsieur LaBatte. I was told that by the woman who came each day to wash their clothes. To want desperately to marry men, I have come to see, is not a mistake women make, it is only, well, what else is left for them to do? I was never told why she wanted to marry him. I made a guess: he had a strong body, she was drawn to his strong body, his strong hands, his strong mouth; it was a big wide mouth and it must have covered hers up whenever he kissed her. It swallowed mine up whenever he kissed me. She was not a frail woman when they first met, she became frail only afterward; he wore her out. When they first met, he would not marry her. He would not marry any woman. They would bear him children, and if the children were boys, these boys were given his full name, but he never married the mothers. Madame LaBatte found a way: she fed him food she had cooked in a sauce made up of her own menstrual blood, which bound him to her, and they were married. In time this spell wore off and could not be made to work again. He turned on her—not in anger, for he never became aware of the trap that had been set for him—he turned on her with the strength of that weapon he carried between his legs, and he wore her out. Her hair was gray, and not from age. Like so much about her it had just lost its vitality, it lay on her head without any real life to it; her hands hung at her side, slack. She had been beautiful when she was young, the way all people are, so beautiful when they are young, but on her face then was the person she had really become: defeated. Defeat is not beautiful; it is not ugly, but it is not beautiful. I was young then; I was young, I did not know. When I looked at her and felt sympathy, I also felt revulsion. I thought, This must never happen to me, and I meant that I would not allow the passage of time or the full weight of desire to make a pawn of me. I was young, so young, and felt my convictions powerfully; I felt strong and I felt I would always be so, I felt new and felt I would always be so, too. And at that moment the clothes I was wearing became too small, my bosoms grew out and pressed against my blouse, my hair touched my shoulders in a caress that caused me to shiver inside, my legs were hot and between them was a moisture, a sweet smelly stickiness. I was alive; I could tell that standing before me was a woman who was not. It was almost as if I sensed a danger and quickly made myself a defense; in seeing the thing I might be, I too early became its opposite.

She liked me. This woman liked me; her husband liked me; it pleased her that he liked me. By the time he emerged from the room where he kept his money, to greet my father and me, Madame LaBatte had already told me to make myself at home, to regard her as if she were my own mother, to feel safe whenever she was near. She could not know what such words meant to me, to hear a woman say them to me. Of course I did not believe her, I did not fool myself, but I knew she meant them when she was saying those things to me, she really meant to say them. I liked her so very much, her shadow of her former self, so grateful for my presence, no longer alone with her prize and her defeat. He did not speak to me right away; he did not care that it was me and not someone else my father had asked him to accommodate. He liked the quiet greed of my father, and my father liked the simple greed in him. They were a match; one could betray the other at any time, perhaps at that moment they already had. Monsieur LaBatte was already a rich man, richer than my father. He had better connections; he had not wasted his time marrying a poor Carib woman for love.

I lived in this household, occupying a room that was attached to the kitchen; the kitchen was not a part of the house itself. I was enjoying the absence of the constant threat posed to me by my father's wife, even as I could feel the burden of my life: the short past, the unknown future. I could write letters to my father, letters that contained simple truths: the days seemed shorter in Roseau than the days in Mahaut, the nights seemed hotter in Roseau than the nights in Mahaut. Madame LaBatte is so very kind to me, she saves as a special treat for me a part of the fish that I love. The part of the fish that I love is the head, something my father would not have known, something I had no reason to believe he wished to know. I sent him these letters without fear. I never received a direct reply; he sent word to me in the letters he wrote to Monsieur LaBatte; he always hoped I was getting along in a good way and he wished me well.

My deep friendship, for it was that, a friendship—perhaps the only one I have ever had—with Madame LaBatte continued to grow. She was always alone. This was true even when she was with others, she was so alone. She thought that she made me sit with her as she sat on the verandah and sewed or just looked out with a blankness at the scene in front of her, but I wanted to sit with her. I was enjoying this new experience, the experience of a silence full of expectation and desire; she wanted something from me, I could tell that, and I longed for the moment to come, the moment that I would know just what it was she wanted. It never crossed my mind that I would refuse her. One day, without any preparation, she gave me a beautiful dress that she no longer wore; it still fit her, but she no longer wore it. As I was trying on the dress I could hear her thoughts: she was thinking of her youth, the person she used to be when she first wore the dress she had just given me, the things she had wanted, the things she had not received, the shallowness of her whole life. All this filled the air in the room we were in, the room in which was the bed she slept in with her husband. My own thoughts answered hers: You were foolish; you should not have let this happen to you. It is your own fault. I was without mercy, my condemnations filled my head with a slow roar until I thought I would faint, and then this thought came upon me slowly, saving me from doing so: She wants to make a gift of me to her husband; she wants to give me to him, she hopes I do not mind. I was standing in this room before her, my clothes coming off, my clothes going on, naked, clothed, but the vulnerability I felt was not of the body, it was of the spirit, the soul. To communicate so intimately with someone, to be spoken to silently by someone and yet understand more clearly than if she had shouted at the top of her voice, was something I did not experience with anyone ever again in my life. I took the dress from her. I did not wear it, I would never wear it; I only took it and kept it for a while.

The inevitable is no less a shock just because it is inevitable. I was sitting, late one day, in a small shaded area behind the house, where some flowers were planted, though this place could not be called a garden, for not much care was applied to it. The sun had not yet set completely; it was just at that moment when the creatures of the day are quiet but the creatures of the night have not quite found their voice. It was that time of day when all you have lost is heaviest in your mind: your mother, if you have lost her; your home, if you have lost it; the voices of people who might have loved you or who you only wish had loved you; the places in which something good, something you cannot forget, happened to you. Such feelings of longing and loss are heaviest just in that light. Day is almost over, night has almost begun. I did not wear undergarments anymore, I found them uncomfortable, and as I sat there I touched various parts of my body, sometimes absentmindedly, sometimes with a purpose in mind. I was running the fingers of my left hand through the small thick patch of hair between my legs and thinking of my life as I had lived it so far, fifteen years of it now, and I saw that Monsieur LaBatte was standing not far off from me, looking at me. He did not move away in embarrassment and I, too, did not run away in embarrassment. We held each other's gaze. I removed my fingers from between my legs and brought them up to my face, I wanted to smell myself. It was the end of the day, my odor was quite powerful. This scene of me placing my hand between my legs and then enjoying the smell of myself and Monsieur LaBatte watching me lasted until the usual sudden falling of the dark, and so when he came closer to me and asked me to remove my clothes, I said, quite sure of myself, knowing what it was I wanted, that it was too dark, I could not see. He took me to the room in which he counted his money, the money that was only some of the money he had. It was a dark room and so he kept a small lamp always lighted in it. I took off my clothes and he took off his clothes. He was the first man I had ever seen unclothed and he surprised me: the body of a man is not what makes him desirable, it is what his body might make you feel when it touches you that is the thrill, anticipating what his body will make you feel, and then the reality becomes better than the anticipation and the world has a wholeness to it, a wholeness with a current running through it, a current of pure pleasure. But when I first saw him, his hands hanging at his side, not yet caressing my hair, not yet inside me, not yet bringing the small risings that were my breasts toward his mouth, not yet opening my mouth wider to place his tongue even deeper in my mouth, the limp folds of the flesh on his stomach, the hardening flesh between his legs, I was surprised at how unbeautiful he was all by himself, just standing there; it was anticipation that was the thrill, it was anticipation that kept me entralled. And the force of him inside me, inevitable as it was, again came as a shock, a long sharp line of pain that then washed over me with the broadness of a wave, a long sharp line of pleasure: and to each piercing that he made inside me, I made a cry that was the same cry, a cry of sadness, for without making of it something it really was not I was not the same person I had been before. He was not a man of love, I did not need him to be. When he was through with me and I with him, he lay on top of me, breathing indifferently; his mind was on other things. On a small shelf at his back I could see he had lined up many coins, their sides turned heads up; they bore the face of a king.

In the room where I slept, the room with the floor of dirt, I poured water into a small tin basin and washed the thin crust of blood that had dried between my legs and down the inside of my legs. This blood was not a mystery to me, I knew why it was there, I knew what had just happened to me. I wanted to see what I looked like, but I could not. I felt myself; my skin felt smooth, as if it had just been oiled and freshly polished. The place between my legs ached, my breasts ached, my lips ached, my wrists ached; when he had not wanted me to touch him, he had placed his own large hands over my wrists and kept them pinned to the floor; when my cries had distracted him, he had clamped my lips shut with his mouth. It was through all the parts of my body that ached that I relived the deep pleasure I had just experienced. When I awoke the next morning I did not feel I had slept at all; I felt as if I had only lost consciousness and I picked up where I had left off in my ache of pleasure.

It had rained during the night, a rain that was beyond torrential, and in the morning it did not stop, in the evening after the morning it did not stop; the rain did not stop for many, many days. It fell with such force and for such a long time that it appeared to have the ability to change the face and the destiny of the world, the world of the outpost Roseau, so that after it stopped, nothing would be the same: not the ground itself that we walked on, not the outcome of even a quarrel. But it was not so; after the rain stopped, the waters formed into streams, the streams ran into rivers, the rivers ran into the sea; the ground retained its shape. I was in a state of upheaval. I would not remain the same, even I could see that; the respectable, the predictable—such was not to be my own destiny.

For the days and nights that the rain fell I could not keep to my routine: make my own breakfast, perform some household tasks in the main house in which Madame and Monsieur lived, then walk to my school, in which all the students were female, shunning their childish company, returning home, running errands for Madame, returning home, performing more household chores, washing my own clothes and generally taking care of my own self and things. I could not attend to any of that; the rain made it impossible.

I was standing in the middle of a smaller version of the larger deluge; it was coming through the roof of my room, which was made of tin. There were the same sensations; I was not used to them yet, but the rain was familiar. A knock at the door, a command; the door shook open. She came to rescue me, she knew how I must be suffering in the wet, she had been in the kitchen and from there she could hear my suffering, caused by this unexpected deluge, this unconscionable downpour; to be alone in it would be the cause of much suffering for me, she could already hear me suffering so. But I was not making a sound at all, only the soft sighs of satisfaction remembered. She took me into the house; she made me coffee, it was hot and strong, with fresh milk he had brought that morning from some cows he kept not too far away from the house. He was not in the house now; he had come and he had gone away. I spent the day with her; I spent the night with him.

It was not an arrangement made with words; it could not be made with words. On that day she showed me how to make him a cup of coffee; he liked to drink coffee with so strong a flavor that it overwhelmed anything that anyone wanted to put in it. She said this: "The taste is so strong you can put anything in it, he would never know." When we were alone we spoke to each other in French patois, the language of the captive, the illegitimate; we never spoke of what we were doing, we never spoke for long, we spoke of the things in front of us and then we were silent. A silence had preceded the instructions to make coffee; a silence followed it. I did not say to her, I do not want to make him coffee, I shall never make him coffee, I do not need to know how to make this man coffee, no man will ever drink coffee from my hands made in that way! I did not say this. She washed my hair and rinsed it with a tea she had made from nettles; she combed it lovingly, admiring its thickness; she applied oil she had rendered from castor beans to my scalp; she plaited it into two braids, just the way I always wore it. She then bathed me and gave me another dress to wear that she had worn when she was a young woman. The dress fit me perfectly, I felt most uncomfortable in it, I could not wait to remove it and put on my own clothes again.

We sat on two chairs, not facing each other, speaking without words, exchanging thoughts. She told me of her life, of the time she went swimming; it was a Sunday, she had been to church and she went swimming and almost drowned, and never did that again, to this day, many years after. It had happened when she was a girl; now she never goes into the water of the sea, she only looks at it; and to my silent question, whether when she looks at the sea she regrets that she is not now part of its everlastingness, she did not answer, she could not answer, so much sadness had overwhelmed her life. The moment she met her Monsieur LaBatte—she called him that then, she called him Jack later, she calls him Him now—she wanted him to possess her. She cannot remember the color of the day. He did not notice her, he did not wish to possess her; his arms were powerful, his lips were powerful, he walked with a purpose, even when he was going nowhere;

she bound him to her, a spell, she wanted to graft herself onto him, the way it's done with trees. She started in the world of the unnatural; she hoped to end in the world of the natural. She wanted only to have him; he would not be had, he would not be contained. To want what you will never have and to know too late that you will never have it is a life overwhelmed with sadness. She wanted a child, but her womb was like a sieve; it would not contain a child, it would not contain anything now. It lay shriveled inside her; perhaps her face mirrored it: shriveled, dried, like a fruit that has lost all its juice. Did I value my youth, did I treasure the newness that was me, sitting next to her in a chair? I did not; how could I? In my loss column, youth had not been entered; in my loss column was my mother; love was not yet in my loss column. I had not yet been loved, I could not tell if the way she had combed my hair was an expression of love. I could not tell if the way she had gently bathed me, passing the piece of cloth over my breasts, between the front and back of my legs, down my thighs, down my calves—if that was love. I could not tell if wanting me dry when I was wet, if wanting me fed when I was hungry—if that was love. I had not had love yet, it was not in my column of gain, so it could not be in my column of loss. The rain fell and we no longer heard it, we would hear only its absence, my days full of silence yet crowded with words, my nights full of sighs, soft and loud with agony and pleasure. I would call out his name, Jack, sometimes like an epithet, sometimes like a prayer. We were never alone together, the three of us; she saw him in one room, I saw him in another. He never spoke to me, not even in silence. He was behaving in a way he knew well, I was following a feeling I had, I was acting from instinct. The feeling I had, the instinct I was acting from, were all new to me. She heard us. She never let me know that she did, that she could hear us. She had wanted a child, had wanted children; I could hear her say that. I was not a child, I could no longer be a child; she could hear me say that. She wanted something again from me, she wanted a child I might have; I did not let her know that I heard that, and this vision she would have, of a child inside me, eventually in her arms, hung in the air like a ghost, something only the special could see. Not for every eye, it was for my eyes, but I would never see it, and it would go away and come back, this ghost of me with a child inside me. I turned my back to it; my ears grew deaf to it; my heart would not beat. She was stitching me a garment from beautiful old cloths she had saved from the different times in her life, the happy times, the sad times. It was a shroud made of memories; how she wished to weave me into its seams, its many seams. How hard she tried; but with each click of the thimble striking the needle, I made an escape. Her frustration and my satisfaction were in their own way palpable.

To become a schoolgirl again was not possible, only I did not know this right away. The climate remained the same, the weather changed. Monsieur went away. I did not see the counting room for a while. In each corner and along the sides of the floor he had small mountains of farthings; on a table he had piled on top of each other more coins, shillings, florins. He had so many coins all over the room, in stacks, that when the lamp was lit, they made the room brighter. In the night I would awake to find him counting his money, over and over, as if he did not know how much he really had, or as if counting would make a difference. He never offered any of it to me, he knew I did not want it, I knew I did not want any of it. The room was not cold or warm or suffocating, but it was not ideal either; I did not want to spend the rest of my life in it. I did not want to spend the rest of my life with the person who owned such a room. When he was not at home, my nights were spent in my room with the dirt floor off the kitchen. My days were spent in a schoolhouse. This education I was receiving had never offered me the satisfaction I was told it would; it only filled me with questions that were not answered, it only filled me with anger. I could not like what it would lead to: a humiliation so permanent that it would replace your own skin. And your own name, whatever it might be, eventually was not the gateway to who you really were, and you could not ever say to yourself, "My name is Xuela Claudette Desvarieux." This was my mother's name, but I cannot say it was her real name, for in a life like hers, as in mine, what is a real name? My own name is her name, Xuela Claudette, and in the place of the Desvarieux is Richardson, which is my father's name; but who are these people Claudette, Desvarieux, and Richardson? To look into it, to look at it, could only fill you with despair; the humiliation could only make you intoxicated with self-hatred. For the name of any one person is at once her history recapitulated and abbreviated, and on declaring it, that person holds herself high or low, and the person hearing it holds the declarer high or low.

My mother was placed outside the gates of a convent when she was perhaps a day old by a woman believed to be her own mother; she was wrapped in pieces of clean old cloth, and the name Xuela was written on these pieces of cloth; it was written in an ink whose color was indigo, a dye rendered from a plant. She was not discovered because she had been crying; even as a newborn she did not draw attention to herself. She was found by a woman, a nun who was on her way to wreak more havoc in the lives of the remnants of a vanishing people; her name was Claudette Desvarieux. She named my mother after herself, she called my mother after herself; how the name Xuela survived I do not know, but my father gave it to me when she died, just after I was born. He had loved her; I do not know how much of the person he was then, sentimental and tender, survived in him.

This moment of my life was an idyll: peace and contentment of innocent young womanhood by day, spent in a large room with other young people of my own sex, all of them the products of legitimate unions, for this school begun by missionary followers of John Wesley did not admit children born outside marriage, and this, apart from everything else, kept the school very small, because most children were born outside marriage. I was surrounded daily by the eventually defeated, the eventually bitter, the dull hum of the voices of these girls; their bodies, already a source of anxiety and shame, were draped in blue sacks made from coarse cotton, a uniform. And then again there were my nights of silences and sighs—all an idyll, and its end I could see even so. I did not know how or when this end would come, but I could see it all the same, and the thought did not fill me with dread.

One day I became very sick. I was with child but I did not know it. I had no experience with the symptoms of such a state and so did not immediately know what was happening to me. It was Lise who told me what was the matter with me. I had just vomited up everything I had ever eaten in my entire life and I felt that I would die, and so I called out her name. "Lise," I said, not Madame LaBatte; she had put me to lie down on her bed; she was lying next to me, holding me in her arms. She said I was "with child"; she said it in English. Her voice had tenderness in it and sympathy, and she said it again and again, that I was having a child, and then she sounded quite happy, smoothing down the hair on my head, rubbing my cheek with the back of her hand, as if I were a baby, too, and in a state of irritation that I could not articulate and her touch would prove soothing to me. Her words, though, struck a terror in me. At first I did not believe her, and then I believed her completely and instantly felt that if there was a child in me I could expel it through the sheer force of my will. I willed it out of me. Day after day I did this, but it did not come out. From deep in Lise's underarms I could smell a perfume. It was made from the juice of a flower, this smell would fill up the room, fill up my nostrils, move down into my stomach and out through my mouth in waves of vomiting; the taste of it slowly strangling me. I believed that I would die, and perhaps because I no longer had a future I began to want one very much. But what such a thing could be for me I did not know, for I was standing in a black hole. The other alternative was another black hole, this other black hole was one I did not know; I chose the one I did not know.

One day I was alone, still lying in Lise's bed; she had left me alone. I got up and walked into Monsieur LaBatte's counting room, and reaching into a small crocus bag that had only shillings in it, I removed from it one handful of this coin. I walked to the house of a woman who is dead now, and when she opened her door to me I placed my handful of shillings in her hands and looked into her face. I did not say a word. I did not know her real name, she was called "Sange-Sange," but that was not her real name. She gave me a cupful of a thick black syrup to drink and then led me to a small hole in a dirt floor to lie down. For four days I lay there, my body a volcano of pain; nothing happened, and for four days after that blood flowed from between my legs slowly and steadily like an eternal spring. And then it stopped. The pain was like nothing I had ever imagined before, it was as if it defined pain itself; all other pain was only a reference to it, an imitation of it, an aspiration to it. I was a new person then, I knew things I had not known before, I knew things that you can know only if you have been through what I had just been through. I had carried my own life in my own hands.

On the road between Roseau and Potter's Ville I was followed by a large agouti whose movements were not threatening. It stopped when I stopped, looked behind itself when I looked behind myself to see what it was up to—I did not know what it saw behind itself—walked when I walked. At Goodwill I stopped to drink water and the agouti stopped but did not drink water then. At Massacre the entire Church of St. Paul and St. Anne was wrapped in purple and black cloth as if it were Good Friday. It was at Massacre that Indian Warner, the illegitimate son of a Carib woman and a European man, was murdered by his half brother, an Englishman named Philip Warner, because Philip Warner did not like having such a close relative whose mother was a Carib woman. I passed through Mahaut crawling on my stomach, for I was afraid I would be recognized. I did not need to swim across the mouth of the Belfast River; the water was low. Just before I reached St. Joseph, at Layou, I spun around three times and called out my name and so made the agouti fall asleep behind me. I never saw it again. It was raining in Merot, it was raining in Coulibistri, it was raining in Colihaut.

I could not see the top of Morne Diablotin; I had never seen it in any case, even when I was awake. At Portsmouth I found bread at the foot of a tree whose fruit was inedible nuts and whose wood is used to make exquisite furniture. I passed by the black waters of the Guadeloupe Channel; I was not tempted to be swallowed up whole in it. Passing through La Haut, passing through Thibaud, passing through Marigot—somewhere between Marigot and Castle Bruce lived my mother's people, on a reserve, as if in commemoration of something no one could bring herself to mention. At Petite Soufrière the road ceased to exist. I passed by the black waters of the Martinique Channel; I was not tempted to be swallowed up whole in it. It rained between Soufrière and Roseau. I believe I heard small rumblings coming from deep within Morne Trois Pitons, I believe I smelled sulfur fumes rising up from the Boiling Lake. And that is how I claimed my birthright, East and West, Above and Below, Water and

Land: In a dream. I walked through my inheritance, an island of villages and rivers and mountains and people who began and ended with murder and theft and not very much love. I claimed it in a dream. Exhausted from the agony of expelling from my body a child I could not love and so did not want, I dreamed of all the things that were mine.

It was the smell coming from my father that awoke me. He had been asked to arrest some men suspected of smuggling rum and they threw stones at him, and when he fell to the ground he was stabbed with a knife. Now he stood over me, and the wound was still fresh; it was on his upper arm, his shirt hid it from sight, but he smelled of iodine and gentian violet and carbolic acid. This smell seemed orderly and reasonable; I associated it with a small room and shelves on which were small brown bottles and bandages and white enamel utensils. This smell reminded me of a doctor. I had once been to a doctor's home; my father had asked me to deliver an envelope inside of which was a piece of paper on which he had written a message. On the envelope he had written the doctor's name: Bailey. This smell he had about him now reminded me of that doctor's room. My father stood over me and looked down. His eyes were gray. He could not be trusted, but you would have to know him for a while to realize that. He did not seem repelled by me. I did not know if he knew what had happened to me. He had been told that I was missing, he looked for me, he found me, he wanted to take me to his home in Mahaut, and when I was well again I could go back to Roseau to live. (He did not say with whom). In his mind he believed he loved me, he was sure that he loved me; all his actions were an expression of this. On his face, though, was that mask; it was the same mask he wore when stealing all that was left from an unfortunate someone who had lost so much already. It was the same mask he wore when he guided an event, regardless of its truth, to an end that would benefit him. And even now, as he stood over me, he did not wear the clothes of a father: he wore his jailer's uniform, he was in his policeman's clothes. And these clothes, these policeman's clothes, came to define him; it was as if eventually they grew onto his body, another skin, because long after he ceased to wear them, when it was no longer necessary for him to wear them, he always looked as if he were still in his policeman's clothes. His other clothes were real clothes; his policeman's clothes had become his skin.

I was lying down on a bed made of rags in a house that had only the bare earth for a floor. There was no real evidence of my ordeal to see. I did not smell of the dead, because for something to be dead, life would have had to come first. I had only made the life that was just beginning in me, not dead, just not to be at all. There was a pain between my legs; it started inside my lower abdomen and my lower back and came out through my legs, this pain. I was wet between my legs; I could smell the wetness; it was blood, fresh and old. The fresh blood smelled like a newly dug-up mineral that had not yet been refined and turned into something worldly, something to which a value could be assigned. The old blood gave off a sweet rotten stink, and this I loved and would breathe in deeply when it came to dominate the other smells in the room; perhaps I only loved it because it was mine. My father was not repelled by me, but I could not see anything else that was written in his face. He stood over me, looking down on me. His face grew round and big, filling up the whole room from one end to the other; his face was like a map of the world, as if a globe had been removed from a dark corner in a sitting room (he owned such things: a globe, a sitting room) after which its main seam had been ripped apart and the globe had been laid open, flat. His cheeks were two continents separated by two seas which joined an ocean (his nose); his gray eyes were bottomless and sleeping volcanoes; between his nose and his mouth lay the equator; his ears were the horizons, to go beyond which was to fall into the thick blackness of nothing; his forehead was a range of mountains known to be treacherous; his chin the area of steppes and deserts. Each area took on its appropriate coloring: the land mass a collection of soft yellows and blues and mauves and pinks, with small lines of red running in every direction as if to deliberately confound; the waters blue, the mountains green, the deserts and steppes brown. I did not know this world, I had only met some of its people. Most of them were not everything you could ask for.

To die then was not something I desired, and I was young enough to believe that this was a choice, and I was young enough for this to be so. I did not die, I did not wish to. I told my father that as soon as I was able to, I would return to the household of Madame and Monsieur LaBatte. My father had a broad back. It was stiff, it was strong; it looked like a large land mass arising unexpectedly out of what had been flat; around it, underneath it, above it I could not go. I had seen this back of his so many times, so many times it had been turned to me, that I was no longer capable of being surprised at the sight of it, but it never ceased to stir up in me a feeling of curiosity: would I see his face again or had I seen him for the last time?

Lise was waiting for me on the steps of the verandah. She had not known when I would show up again, or if I would show up again, but she had waited for me, she *was* waiting for me. She wore a new black dress with an old piece of crushed-up cloth pinned just above her left bosom. The color of the cloth was red, an old red that had only darkened with time. She said, "My dear," only that, "My dear," and she wrapped her arms around me and drew me close to her. I could not feel her; even as she pressed me close to her, I could not feel her. She drew away from me, she could hear her husband's footsteps coming along the path. He was wearing his galoshes, I could tell. I knew the sound of his footsteps when his feet were in his galoshes. When he saw me, he did not mention that I had been away; I knew that if he had noticed, he would not tell me in any case. I did not care, I was curious. We stood, the three of us, in a little triangle, a trinity, not made in heaven, not made in hell, a wordless trinity. And yet at that moment someone was of the defeated, someone was of the resigned, and someone was changed forever. I was not of the defeated; I was not of the resigned. There was a castor-oil bush growing, untended by human hand, not far from us, and I fixed my eyes on it with a hard stare, for I wanted to remember to harvest the seeds when they became ripe, render the oil from them, and drink it to clean out my insides.

My heart was not unmoved by the sight of Lise haunting the space of ground that stood between the house in which she lived and the small hut I occupied. She swept the ground at night, in the dark when it rained; she planted small bushes that bore white flowers, then uprooted them and put in their place some lilies that would eventually bear flowers the color of the inside of an orange. How long it would take for the orange-colored flowers to appear she did not know, but she was very sure they would please me. She wore the black dress with the tattered red flower over her breast day after day. She was in mourning. Her eyes were black and shiny with tears; the tears were trapped there, they never spilled out. Her arms would reach out to me—I never stood too near her—then up to the wide-open blue sky as if she were drowning, her mouth open with no sound coming out, yet even so I could hear her say, "Save me, save me"; but even if she did not know, I knew it was not herself she wanted to save; it was me she wanted to consume. I was not unmoved by the sight of her, she was a sad sight to me; but I was not an angel, nothing in me broke.

I could hear the clap of thunder, the roar of water falling from great heights into great pools and the great pool wending its way slowly toward the sea; I could hear clouds emptying themselves of their moisture as if by accident, as if someone had kicked over a goblet in the dark, and their contents landing on an indifferent earth; and I could hear the silence and I could hear the dark night gobbling it up, and it in turn being gobbled up by the light of yet another day.

My father wrote to my host and hostess to ask after my health; he did not know what had happened to me and so he asked them to forgive me the bad manners I had shown when I disappeared without telling them of my whereabouts, and went to live all by myself in a section of Roseau which was dangerous and unsanitary, and so almost caused my own death. He sent me his best through them. He sent me five guineas. Lise gave me the five guineas. She showed me the letter. His handwriting was such a beautiful thing to behold. It covered the page with strong curves and strong dashes and strong slashes. I could not read it; I could not bring myself to make out each word and put them together in sentences. I only saw that his handwriting covered the page from top to bottom. The envelope bore the postmark of Dublanc, a small town in the parish of St. Peter, many, many miles away from Roseau; even so, I felt I knew the small miseries he had created and left in his wake there.

The days followed the nights with a helpless regularity, day devouring night devouring day devouring night with such obsessiveness that it might have fascinated me if I could be fascinated. I wanted time to pass in one fell swoop, like the blink of an eye; I wanted to look up and suddenly find myself looking at the events of my immediate past on a horizon from which I was receding rapidly. When this did not become so, I did not grow insane, I did not grow tired. I left the household of the LaBattes at the very blackest point of the night. This was not because of the cover of darkness. I did not want the actual sight of Lise seeing me leave her to haunt me for the rest of my life; I could imagine it well enough. I walked just past the village of Loubière and rented a house for which I paid sixpence a week. I had four dresses, two pairs of shoes, a very nice straw hat, and the five guineas given to me by my father; it was not nothing. A road was being built between Loubière and Giraudel. I took a job sifting the sand needed for it. I was paid eightpence for each day of work, and each day of work consisted of ten hours; at the end of a fortnight I received in a small brown envelope my pay of seven shillings and fourpence.

In this house, for which I paid sixpence a week, I spent all my time that I was not working. I acquired bedding, a mattress stuffed with coconut fiber, from a woman who lived in the middle of the village. It was not new; I could not tell if she was the only one who had slept on it before, but I was not afraid to take on the hardships of all who had done so. My life was beyond empty. I had never had a mother, I had just recently refused to become one, and I knew then that this refusal would be complete. I would never become a mother, but that would not be the same as never bearing children. I would bear children, but I would never be a mother to them. I would bear them in abundance; they would emerge from my head, from my armpits, from between my legs; I would bear children, they would hang from me like fruit from a vine, but I would destroy them with the carelessness of a god. I would bear children in the morning, I would bathe them at noon in a water that came from myself, and I would eat them at night, swallowing them whole, all at once. They would live and then they would not live. In their day of life, I would walk them to the edge of a precipice. I would not push them over; I would not have to; the sweet voices of unusual pleasures would call to them from its bottom; they would not rest until they became one with these sounds. I would cover their bodies with diseases, embellish skins with thinly crusted sores, the sores sometimes oozing a thick pus for which they would thirst, a thirst that could never be quenched. I would condemn them to live in an empty space frozen in the same posture in which they had been born. I would throw them from a great height; every bone in their body would be broken and the bones would never be properly set, healing in the way they were broken, healing never at all. I would decorate them when they were only corpses and set each corpse in a polished wooden box, and place the polished wooden box in the earth and forget the part of the earth where I had buried the box. It is in this way that I did not become a mother; it is in this way that I bore my children.

In that house with its openings of one door and three windows, the many crevices in the sides where the planks of wood did not meet, the holes in its roof made from the branches of a coconut tree, I sat, I stood, I lay down at night, and so sealed the doom of the children I would never have. I slept; the dawn came; I went to work; the dusk fell. Each morning I roasted coffee beans, pounded them into a coarse powder, and brewed a beverage that was thick and black and so pungent the flavor of it caused my taste buds to feel not whole but as if they had been stripped and flung about into various parts of my atmosphere.

I did not yet know how vulnerable each individual is to the small eruptions that establish themselves inside her heart. I bought from his wife the garments of a man who had just died: his old nankeen drawers, his one old pair of khaki pants, his old shirt of some kind of cotton. I paid her fourpence for all this, plus a hand of bananas and some ground food. It was these clothes, the clothes of a dead man, that I wore to work each day. I cut off the two plaits of hair on my head; they fell to my feet looking like two headless serpents. I wrapped my almost hairless head in a piece of old cloth. I did not look like a man, I did not look like a woman. Each morning I cooked the food I would eat at midday; I wrapped it in fig leaves, then wrapped it again in a knapsack made out of a tired piece of madras cloth and took it with me to work. All day I carried buckets filled with black sand, or filled with mud, or filled with small stones; all day I dug holes and filled the holes with water and bailed water out of other holes. I spoke to no one, not even to myself. Inside me there was nothing; inside me there was a vault made of a substance so heavy I could find nothing to compare it to; and inside the vault was an ache of such intensity that each night as I lay alone in my house all my exhalations were long, low wails, like a lanced boil, with a small line of pus trickling out, not like a dam that had burst.

I came to know myself, and this frightened me. To rid myself of this fear I began to look at a reflection of my face in any surface I could find: a still pool on the shallow banks of the river became my most common mirror. When I could not see my face, I could feel that I had become hard; I could feel that to love was beyond me, that I had gained such authority over my own ability to be that I could cause my own demise with complete calm. I knew, too, that I could cause the demise of others with the same complete calm. It was seeing my own face that comforted me. I began to worship myself. My black eyes, the shape of half-moons, were alluring to me; my nose, half flat, half not, as if painstakingly made that way, I found so beautiful that I saw in it a standard which the noses of the people I did not like failed to meet. I loved my mouth; my lips were thick and wide, and when I opened my mouth I could take in volumes, pleasure and pain, awake or asleep. It was this picture of myself—my eyes, my nose, my mouth set in the seamless, unwrinkled, unblemished skin which was my face—that I willed before me. My own face was a comfort to me, my own body was a comfort to me, and no matter how swept away I would become by anyone or anything, in the end I allowed nothing to replace my own being in my own mind.

It was in this way that I lived, alone and yet with everything and everyone that I had been and had known, and would be and would know, apart from my present—and yet to be apart from my present was impossible. One day I saw my father. He saw me also. Our eyes did not meet. We did not speak words to each other. He was riding a donkey. He was wearing his jailer's uniform, the same one he always wore, khaki shirt and khaki pants, so well ironed; only, on the shoulder of his shirt there was a new green-and-yellow stripe. It meant he had been elevated to new levels of authority. He was bearing a summons for someone; his presence as always was a sign of misfortune. Wherever he was, someone was bound to have less than they'd had before my father made an appearance.

He looked so much as if he were born that way: erect; back stiff and straight, lips held tightly together, eyes clear as if they had never been clouded with tears, footsteps never faltering; even the beasts he rode never stumbled. He did not look as if he had ever been a baby and caused anyone to worry that he would die in the middle of the night of a fever, a cough, the breath suddenly leaving his body and never returning. To grow powerful became him, and as he grew more powerful, he did not grow fat and slovenly; he grew sleek, finely honed. You had to look into his eyes to see what he was made of, something deeply satisfying to him; and he would not tell you what that was, you had to look into his eyes. His eyes were the first thing everyone wanted to see about him; and people who saw him for the first time, who did not know him at all, looked for his eyes without thinking that they wanted to see them.

He was making a visit to the site at which I worked. He came to where I was sitting, taking a short break from my labor, and left a bundle at my side. I did not open it immediately, I took it to my house and opened it that night. His gift to me was one Ugli fruit and three grapefruit. I remembered then that once, when I was a child, he had taken me to ground with him, wanting to show me the new land he had just acquired, which conveniently adjoined his old property. Without knowing why, I held my young self away from my inheritance, for that was what was being shown to me. On the new land he had planted many young grapefruit trees, and showing it all to me with a wide sweep of his hand—a gesture more appropriate to a man richer than he was, a gesture of all-encompassing ownership—he told me that the grapefruit was natural to the West Indies, that sometime in the seventeenth century it had mutated from the Ugli fruit on the island of Jamaica. He said this in a way that made me think he wanted the grapefruit and himself to be One. I did not know what was on his mind at the time he told me this.

After I had been living in this way for a very long time, not a man, not a woman, not anything, not gathering, only living through my past, sifting it, trying to forget some things and never succeeding, trying to keep the memory of others more strongly alive and never succeeding, I received a letter from my father asking me to come home to his house in Mahaut. The letter was given to me by a man I had never seen before, but from his bowed head I could tell that my father knew him very well. The letter was dated two days earlier; I noticed this because only the day before I had seen my father, appearing in his usual way as a despised official, bearing documents which would lead to the imprisonment of some, the permanent impoverishment of others; he could have given me the letter himself then. His handwriting, like the rest of him, had been overtaken by officialdom. I remembered seeing the letters from him Lise and Jack received when I was living with them, and his handwriting then was more rounded, climbing up and down the page unevenly, the "Dear Jack and Madame La Batte" very large, taking up all of the first line, his "Your friend" just barely squeezing in at the bottom of the page. Not so the handwriting of this letter asking me to return to his house. The letters had been formed with a very hard and expensive pen nib, the ink was a thick unwatery black, the writing was the kind to be seen on an official document. The paper was a soft cream, the lines on it thin and green. All it lacked was a governmental seal. My brother was very sick, he wrote, and might die soon; my sister had developed into a sour personality and had been sent to school in Roseau, where she also lived with some nuns even though we were not Roman Catholics; my stepmother had grown distant from him. He wrote that:

my brother, my sister, my stepmother; but I substituted these words: your son, your daughter, your wife. They were his; they were not mine. He wanted to tell me that we were all his; it was at that moment that I felt I did not want to belong to anyone, that since the one person I would have consented to own me had never lived to do so, I did not want to belong to anyone; I did not want anyone to belong to me.

A wild bush had been in bloom for many days now. As I read the letter I looked at it. Its many flowers were small and a deep pink, with long deep throats and short flared lips for petals. A single bee kept going in and coming out, going in and coming out, in a leisurely fashion, as if it was at play, not at work at all. I suddenly grew tired of the life I had been leading; it had served its purpose. I suddenly felt I did not want to wear the clothes of a dead man anymore. I took off my clothes and set fire to them. I bathed myself. I wanted to set fire to the house I had lived in all this time before I left it, but I did not want to bring attention to my absence; I did not want anyone to notice that I had been there and that now I was not.

I left for my father's house in the middle of the night. This was not by design; I was ready to leave just then. I packed everything I owned into a small bundle and placed it on my head. It was not very heavy, it was not very much. The things I had had when I came I still had, except I had more money, and this I had worked very hard for. When I left, the night was black, a moon was in the sky, but I could not see it: a thick cloud hung a false ceiling between us. I was alone. My feet knew the road as if I had made it myself. By morning I was passing through Roseau. I did not stop. My father's daughter was there. Lise and Jack were there. They did not interest me in the least. I did not wonder what they were both doing just then.

It was before I reached Massacre that I passed a woman who was not much older than I was but who looked twice my age. I recognized her as someone who used to come to my father's house and help his wife to wash their clothes and sweep their yard. She did not perform this duty of washing clothes for me; his wife did not wish it, I would not allow it, I wanted to do everything for myself. At that moment I was seeing her she resembled a martyr, but to what I am quite certain she had no idea. She walked with her hands folded in front of her, resting on her stomach. Her stomach was swollen, but I could not tell whether it was with child or from illness. Her dress was old and faded and needed washing. Her feet were without shoes. Her hair was uncombed. Her skin, which when I first knew her had been a fresh black, as if its blackness had just been newly made, was now dull and tired, and nothing could refresh it. We passed each other exactly under the canopy of an old tree; the earth had been torn away from its roots by so many rains that the roots were exposed in a merciless way to the elements: half of the tree was alive, half of it was dead. Neither this woman nor the tree became a symbol of anything to me. I had come to know that I would rather be all dead or all alive, but never half of one and half of the other at the same time.

When I saw my father's house again, I wept. It was situated at the far end of the village of Mahaut if you were coming from Roseau, going toward Belmont. I had never realized that it was a beautiful house outside, its wood frame painted yellow with deep brown windows. These shades of brown and yellow were not beautiful in themselves and yet they were beautiful when seen on this house. It was across the road from the sea, the big sea, so silvery, so without end, so blue, so all-encompassing, so gray, so without mercy, so powerful and without thought. Against this, the house was so delicate, so vulnerable to the force of the sea that it faced, for it was not unreasonable to think that from time to time the waves of the sea could reach it. It was not an old house; it had been built according to my father's instructions, but already it sagged with the many burdens of its inhabitants: my father's grief for the loss of my mother; his marriage to his present wife, whom he had not loved for herself but for her family's connections and wealth; the grief her own barrenness had caused her; his son's lack of good health; the waywardness of his younger daughter. I could not see anything of myself in this house; I could see only others. I did not belong in it. I did not yet belong anywhere.

My father's daughter whom he had had with his wife who was not my mother was born in the middle of the day, when the sun was directly overhead, and that was not a good thing. It was too bright a time of day to be born; to be born at such a time could only mean that you would be robbed of all your secrets, your ability to determine events. No room could be made dark enough to protect you from a brutality so spare, so voluptuous: life itself. The time of day when his son was born did not matter at all. Any time of day a son is born is the right time. At the time his son was born my father was no longer in love with life itself; he was not in love with anything. He only wanted more of everything, and of the everything he wanted, he did not want to wear it on himself. He did not want people to look at the coat he was wearing and know that he had many more where that came from; he wanted the things that could be laid at his feet, he wanted things he could do without, he wanted things that were without real use. Perhaps this was because in his life he had already exhausted the experience of usefulness, the experience of needing, the idea of desire. He was an animal of neutrality. He could absorb love; he could absorb hate. He could go on. His passions were his own: they did not obey a law of reason, they did not obey a law of passionate belief, and yet he could be described as reasonable, as someone of passionate beliefs. I was like him. I was not like my mother who was dead. I was like him. He was alive.

Inside that yellow house with the brown windows, my father's son was lying on a bed of clean rags that was on the floor. They were special rags; they had been perfumed with oils rendered from things vegetable and animal. It was to protect him from evil spirits. He was on the floor so that the spirits could not get to him from underneath. His mother believed in obeah. His father held the beliefs of the people who had subjugated him. He was not dead; he was not alive. That he was not one or the other was not his fault: to be brought into the world is not ever anyone's responsibility, the decision is never your own. He in particular was someone else's idea. He was an idea of his own mother to make his father forget the woman he had loved before. To make someone forget another person is impossible. Someone can forget an event, someone can forget an item, but no one can ever forget someone else.

And so my father's son lay, his body covered with small sores, his entire being not dead, not alive. It was said that he had yaws; it was said that he was possessed by an evil spirit that caused his body to sprout sores. His father believed one remedy would cure him, his mother believed in another; it was their beliefs that were at odds with each other, not the cures themselves. My father prayed to make him well, but his prayers were like an incitement to the disease: small lesions grew larger, the flesh on his left shin slowly began to vanish as if devoured by an invisible being, revealing the bone, and then that also began to vanish. His mother called in a man who dealt in obeah and a woman who dealt in obeah who were native to Dominica, and then she sent for a woman, a native of Guadeloupe; it was said that someone crossing seawater with a cure would have more success. The disease was indifferent to every principle; no science, no god of any kind could alter its course, and after he died, his mother and father came to believe that his death was inevitable from the beginning.

He died. His name was Alfred; he was named after his father. His father, my father, was named after Alfred the Great, the English king, a personage my father should have despised, for he came to know this Alfred not through the language of the poet, which would have been the language of compassion, but through the language of the conqueror. My father was not responsible for his own name, but he was responsible for the name of his son. His son's name was Alfred. My father perhaps imagined a dynasty. It was laughable only to someone excluded from its substance, someone like me, someone female; anyone else would understand entirely. He had imagined himself as continuing to live on through the existence of someone else. My father had never suffered the indignity of coming upon his own reflection in some shiny surface by accident and finding it so compelling that he came to believe that his own reflection was his soul also. He thought his son looked like him, and perhaps he did, though I would never have thought so; he thought his son was just like him, and perhaps he really was, but this son of his did not live long enough for me to draw such a conclusion.

My brother died. In death he became my brother. When he was alive, I did not know him at all. His hair was black like his mother's. His eyes were brown like hers also. He was kind, he was gentle, but it was the kindness and gentleness of the weak, not out of largesse, not out of instinct. He had a great beauty, but he did not make you want to touch him, not because he repelled you, but because he made you afraid that just to touch him would be to cause him harm, as if he were something vegetable and out of a fable. My father loved him: he was good; he would inherit much; the foul work of acquiring would be unknown to him. How he would keep his inheritance is a thought that would occur and be an irritation only to someone like myself, the disenchanted, and, before that, the disinherited. His father loved him; their names were the same: Alfred. This boy died. Before he died, from his body came a river of pus. Just as he died, a large brown worm crawled out of his left leg; it lay there, above the ankle, as if waiting to be found by a wanderer one morning. It soon dried up and then looked as if all life had left its body thousands of years before. They became inseparable then, my brother and the worm that emerged from his body just as he died. My father did not stop living then, nor did he lose the desire to continue living, he only came to believe that there was a secret purpose to all his suffering and he longed for it to be revealed to him.

My brother died and the seas were still, but not in the usual way; the wind did not blow, the leaves of the trees were still, the earth did not shake, the rivers did not swell, the sky was blue in that eternally deceptive way—innocent, as if it could never change; everything was itself, just the way it would be no matter what happened, but the world had changed for my father, and I believe now that he felt small again, insignificant, helpless against life itself taking a course indifferent to his own wishes. A sheen of calm came over him then, the sheen of calm that is seen in a saint, but I am sure no real saint ever looks like that; it is something seen only in paintings.

My brother was buried in the churchyard of the Methodist church in Roseau. His mother was silent in her grief; she had longed for something also. It centered around her son, his importance; his strength and accomplishments would be a source of pride to her. He looked like her; his beauty was her beauty also. So closely did she see herself tied up with him that when he died, she felt she had died, too; she could not bring herself to actually die; she could be among the living only in body, her spirit now was with her dead son. I felt sorry for her then but not enough to forgive and forget that she had once tried to make me dead also, and most certainly always wished me dead and would make me dead if she could ever bring herself alive enough to accomplish this. Hymns were sung, prayers were offered; they were prayers asking for forgiveness and they were prayers acknowledging an acceptance of events that were ultimately disappointing. But such is the lot of the defeated: in the end what is was meant to be, in the end the other outcome, the outcome of triumph, would have been a tragedy, a consequence far more devastating than the defeat being experienced now. Such is the consolation of the defeated.

My father and his wife and his daughter, the girl who was not me, his wife who was her mother, formed a triangle of pain, of blame, of suspicion, of revenge. To my father none of it had a personal, intimate nature. He did not quarrel with his wife. She, too, was now a source of disappointment. I was only a reminder of disappointment, on the one hand; on the other, I was of the flesh of someone he believed he had loved. My father could not love, but he believed he could, and that must be enough, because perhaps half the world feels that way. He believed he loved me, but I could tell him how untrue that was, I could list for him the number of times he had placed me squarely within the jaws of death; I could list for him the number of times he had failed to be a father to me, his motherless child, while on his way to becoming a man of this world. He loved, he loved; he loved himself. It is perhaps the way of all men. Having lost that small vessel through which he had hoped to perpetuate himself, he then became his own legacy. He was his own future. When he died the world would cease to exist.

To his daughter, the one who was not me, my presence was such an irritant that even when I was not standing in front of her she arranged her face in the disfiguring frown she had created solely for me. She insisted that I was not my father's child, and that even if I was his child, I was illegitimate. The look of awe and bewilderment that alternately crossed her face when she realized that I welcomed this characterization made me pity her. I wished somehow she would draw inspiration from me. Why am I not valued? is the question she wanted to ask the world, the world as constituted by her mother and her father; but she could not ask such a question, she could not begin to suspect there might be an answer. Her mother could not look at her, for what a waste she was, she was the wrong one to be alive. Her father had never really looked at her; seeing her after his son died was not so different from seeing her before he had died. Her mother now greeted her always with silence. Her father continued never speaking to her at all.

She became my sister when shortly after she was expelled from school she found herself with child and I helped her rid herself of this condition. It was not hard to do; I had remembered everything from my own experience. She did not want anything surrounding these events to be advertised, so I hid her in my small room behind the kitchen where I had resumed living. I still cooked my own food. I made her strong potions of teas. When the child inside her still refused to come out, I put my hand up into her womb and forcibly removed it. She bled for days. Her body shrank and crumpled up with pain. She did not die. I had become such an expert at being ruler of my own life in this one limited regard that I could extend such power to any other woman who asked me for it. But my sister did not ask me for it. I never became *her* sister; she never took me into her confidence, she never thanked me; in fact, the powerful clasp in which she could see I held my own life only led to more suspicion and misunderstanding.

She was expelled from her school for having a clandestine relationship with a man; it had been described just that way by the headmistress in a letter to our father: Elizabeth has been conducting a clandestine relationship with a young policeman from St. Joseph. This letter lay on a table in that room of my father's house in which everything looked as if it had been plucked from a picture—a painting, not a photograph, so lustrous, so lifelike, yet so dead. Nothing in the world could have made me resist reading it. It said, Cher Monsieur et Chère Madame, and the rest was in English. My sister had a row with herself, for her mother did not speak to her and her father had never spoken to her. She denied everything. She made up a story that gave me my first insight into the life of childhood and what a real child might say and do. A child looks at the horizon and believes that the world is flat and that when you get to the edge you will fall off into nothingness. Such a belief is a child's belief. It is not a scientific explanation that makes such a belief laughable; it is the lack of faith, the lack of complexity that makes it so. She believed with all her might that her explanations were transparently true: she had climbed over the wall of the convent to take a walk because the enclosed atmosphere caused her to feel homesick and she missed the openness of her dear Mahaut so; each time she escaped the walls of the convent in the middle of the night, by a strange coincidence she met the same man, a Claude Pacquet, a young man who hoped one day to be a bailiff. Such silliness was laughable only if you lived in a large, comfortable world in which your family's position could not be questioned, in which your own position could not be questioned. Her mother did not laugh. Her father did not laugh. I did not laugh.

When she was fully recovered from expelling the child she did not want from her body, the very first thing she did was to spit at the ground in front of me after saying words she thought would do a great injury to my feelings. But even when I was born I was older than her seventeen years of age, so her words did not come as a surprise. I had not expected gratitude, though I would have welcomed it. I had not expected friendship; that I would have regarded with suspicion. The empty space in the small yellow house that had always been her home she could not fill. She looked so much like her father, more so than her brother had: her skin was the same as his, a mixture of people—not races, people—her hair, red and gold and tightly curled, had the texture of hair on the back of a sheep; her eyes were gray, like the moon when seen against a navy-blue sky, and yet she was not beautiful; it was not in her character, beauty. She was fierce; she had been born feeling that her birthright was already spoken for. She thought I was the person who might take it away from her. I could not. I was not a man.

Her father, my father, had by this time become a very rich man. This was unusual for a man of his standing, a native; that is, a man who through blood is associated with the African people. His wealth was a wonder to other people who could be labeled native. These other people, the natives, had become bogged down in issues of justice and injustice, and they had become attached to claims of ancestral heritage, and the indignities by which they had come to these islands, as if they mattered, really mattered. Not so my father. He had a view of things, of history, of time, as if he had lived through many ages, and what he might have seen was that in the short run everything mattered and in the long run nothing mattered. It would all end in nothing, in death, as if you had never been there, and no matter how glorious your presence had been, if at any given moment no one cared about it enough to die for it, enough to live for it, it did not matter at all. Everything mattered, and then again, nothing mattered. He grew rich and rich again. He did not wear it on himself. He did not wear gold, he did not wear silver. He wore a fine white linen suit, so well tailored to fit him—it was not his skin but it could have been. He looked magnificent: a bird of prey, an insect vulnerable to a bird of prey, a master of the jungle, a ruler of the plain, a small mammal. His skin then began to wrinkle, the folds were tiny, creases so minute that only someone as interested as I would have noticed.

My sister did not notice. Her father's wealth did not seem unusual to her. He should be rich, she should be his daughter. She bought a comb—I did not know from where—that when heated and run through her own tightly curled hair made it lie flat against her head. It gleamed in the sunlight, piles and piles of it, like a kind of wealth. Her father was a thin man. He never ate food in a way to suggest he enjoyed it. Her waist grew wide, her hips wider. Her bosoms were large but without seductive appeal; they grew larger, but they did not invite caresses. Ah, how much she did not know herself caused me such sadness that for one whole day I wept from it. She, too, was in love with herself, but hers was not a self worth loving.

And one day my father got a motorcar. It was not a new car, it had belonged to someone else, but that did not matter; he had a car. In it he and his wife and his daughter would drive to Roseau each Sunday and attend church. They would drive back and eat a large meal, sometimes by themselves, sometimes with a man he had befriended, a man who was from England. I did not go in the car with them to church, I did not go to church at all, and I did not eat dinner with them. My sister had been given a bicycle; it was a luxury, not a thing common to everyone. After this Sunday meal, which was made up of meat cooked in the English style, roasted, and a collection of starches, some sweet, some savory, called puddings, she would go out on her bicycle for a ride. A ride to where? I immediately knew that it was a ride to be in the company of the man from St. Joseph. It is possible that her mother and father knew this also, but they did not mention it, they did not speak to her anymore, certainly not to give her a warning. For many Sunday afternoons she took a ride on her bicycle, and when she left her parents' house it was with an idea that they all agreed upon: enjoyment of a specific kind. She would ride through the pleasant afternoon air, the heat lessening as the day grew shorter, the light softening as the day grew shorter, all enthusiasm that began with the long yawn of the morning dampening as the day grew shorter. But the heat, the light, the length of the day held no importance for her; she was going to meet a man. Her mother and my father knew this, that she was going to meet a man, and that it was that man, the very one from St. Joseph, the one they did not like. They had by that time exhausted their ability to oppose: they had opposed the dying of their son, and death had come to him anyway.

It had grown dark one Sunday when she was returning from her clandestine meeting with him. They had met in a place between Massacre and Roseau, they had kissed, he had been on top of her, they were both half clothed, she had gasped, he had groaned, she had said to him that she loved him, he had not said such a thing to her, but she did not notice; he had withdrawn himself from her, she still clung to him. The way he pleased her when he was inside her, his body just that part between his waist and his knees, moving away from her as if forever and then inside her as if forever, was so glorious to my sister that she thought this sensation was unique to her being with him; she did not know she could have this sensation with anyone else, including her own self. She was in love with him, and what did that mean? It was something I hoped never to know, for she made it look like the definition of foolishness itself. She was rounding the bend on her bicycle, the sharp bend, the bend that was so sharp it felt that way even when you were walking slowly, returning from her meeting with him that Sunday afternoon. She was going at too fast a pace and she went off the road, falling over the precipice into the tops of some trees and then onto the tops of some rocks, the small remains of a volcanic eruption. That she was alive after this was considered a miracle, which was true, and a blessing, but her survival seemed a blessing only to all who could not imagine and so therefore had faith in the future.

I had seen her Sunday afternoon before she set out to meet her destiny and she had had that peculiar way about her that people sometimes get, which I now know but did not at the time: that look which says, Every action I now take is the action that will determine my end. She had quarreled with herself, though she thought she had just had a disagreement with her mother, but her mother was not paying attention to her at all. She wore a white dress made of cotton; her father insisted on her wearing white on Sunday, not because of any custom recognizable to anyone, but only because he had an idea of his own virtue and it was superior to other people's virtue and recognizable only to himself. As she went to fetch her bicycle, she had met me, and she had looked at me in a way that was to become the set look of her features: the corners of her lips upturned; the irises of her eyes strained to the far corners, rendering the object at which she was gazing out of focus. A bitterness came out of her nostrils; it was not the air she breathed in but the air she exhaled. She was without pity when she looked at me, but it did not matter, I did not need her pity. When I saw her again she was lying in a bed in the hospital in Roseau. She was alone then. Her father had been there before me, her mother had been there before me, they had not been there before at the same time. It had been ten days; she had fallen off the precipice ten days earlier. The strangeness of life had not yet occurred to her, the short-livedness of each moment, each day, each existence itself, had not yet occurred to her; I do not now believe it ever has. I believe that at the end of her life she was unhappy, she was confused—exactly as she had been at the beginning. Life is of course not a mystery, everyone born knows only too well its entire course; the mystery is a trick designed for the cursedly curious.

She was lying in between the coarse sheets of the hospital bed. Her skin was a pale brown, like new paper, the deep brown pigment lying on top. She was beyond being happy or unhappy to see me. She could not see me clearly at all. I perhaps looked like three or one hundred people to her; whether I was three or one hundred, she still did not like me at all. But she would never like the world again. I had come to see her of my own free will. It had not been expected of me; no one had asked me to do it. When she saw me, she turned her head away; perhaps it was from disgust, or perhaps she was ashamed.

When I saw her lying in a bed in a small room in which there were six other beds but no other patients, a man was standing over her. He was the same man who sometimes came to have dinner with my father and my father's wife on a Sunday; he was the same man with whom I would spend the longest part of my life, but how was I to know that then? She did not look up at me, she did not want to see me; he looked at me, but at that moment I held no significance for him, and later he did not remember that he had seen me then. When she looked at me, she saw me as if I were replicated ten times, each partially imposed upon another, and no version of me fully revealed. This sight of me made her feel uncertain; she turned away from me in anger. I should have loved her then, enough to quell the curiosity that was aroused in me when I saw her lying there: what was he like, he who could bring her to this, a semi-invalid whose vision would forever be blurred?

My father had taken the world as he found it and made it subject to his whims, even as other men had made him subject to their whims in the world as they had found it. He had never questioned these worlds within worlds, not as far as I knew. He was a rich man; there were men richer than he was, and men richer than that. They would all come to the same end, nothing could save them. He had lived long enough to have lost faith in his efforts, to have lost the belief that they had some future value, but his dabbling in the material gain of this world was like a drug: he was addicted to it, he could not just give it up. His heir only his wife's daughter now—his son was dead, his wife was dead, I had removed myself from such a position—had no connection to his feelings about the makeup of the world, and might not by nature have his same feelings about the world in any case; she only saw her father's fortune as freeing her from the burden of the everyday life she saw around her: a life of sweeping ground that would shortly only be dirty again; a life of cooking food that would only be consumed, with more food needing to be cooked again; of making clothes clean that would only be worn and be dirtied and need to be cleaned again. And yet perhaps my father was correct to pursue the world, and my sister correct to enjoy it, because its opposite, the pursuit of death, is not a pursuit at all: death is the inevitable of all inevitables, the only certainty in every uncertainty.

And so I went to meet the man who had brought my sister to the bottom of a precipice, lying in a hospital bed, a semi-invalid for the rest of her life. He had never visited her in the hospital, perhaps he had not heard of her accident. She believed he had not; she certainly believed he had not; the messengers were not people she knew; they were not reliable. I was the one person who could get a message to him, but to beg such a thing of me was too humbling, to have me know that he had refused her wish was more than she could bear. I went to see him all the same. He was a vain man, but his vanity was of the ordinary kind; it did not come from some secret belief, some deep knowledge of himself, it came from something he believed other people saw when they looked at him, something in the way he carried himself, in the intense and compelling way he fixed his gaze on them, a certain gait he had in his walk. If I could have been amused, if I could have had time in my life for laughter, such a person as he was could have provided it.

He had a mustache, a thick, sharp brush of bristles, which he caressed with the fingers of his left hand, no matter what the situation. I had already put the neck of my dress over my head, my arms through my sleeves; I was just putting my belt through its buckle when I told him that my sister was in the hospital, she had suffered an accident, and she longed to see him. He did not know Elizabeth had a sister, and when I asked him how would knowing such a thing have changed his world, he played with his mustache and laughed; it was a sound only he could hear. His hands had been incapable of providing pleasure, or even providing interest; his lips were wide and generous, they satisfied themselves. When I had left my sister's bedside to go to see him, I was driven by curiosity, but it was not a curiosity of any intensity. In the end I wanted to see if it was not too late to dissuade her from making permanent the presence of this unworthy man in her life; in the end I did not care, and in the end again, it did not matter anyway.

They were married, but years passed before the event took place: three, four, five, six, then seven. She was never well again after the accident. Her entire body was so marked by scars that it looked like a map on which the lines had been drawn and redrawn, the result of battles whose outcomes were never final. For a time she wept for days and nights. Then she stopped and never cried again. She waited. One day, not too long into her seven-year wait, a woman came to my father's house and asked for my sister. When my sister came to her she pushed a small bundle into her arms and said that in the bundle was a child; she was its mother and Pacquet was its father. She then vanished. My sister and I took care of the child, though in reality it was I who did so, tending to its needs, for she was incapable of taking care of herself, much less a small child. The child did not thrive, and after two years it died of a disease said to be whooping cough. The child's life passed unnoticed, as if it had never happened. My father forbade its burial in the same graveyard as his son, Alfred. In the end it was buried among a small sect of Christian believers, a sect my father did not think too much of.

I was not invited to their wedding. There was nothing unusual about the day on which they were married. It rained on and off, the sky was the color of milk just let from a cow into an old pail; nothing held a portent of good or ill. Everything was indifferent to this match-up. My sister wore a dress of white silk; it came from far away, it came from China, but it was said that she was married in English silk. She wore pearls around her neck; my father had given them to her mother, I do not know from where he got them. She was beside herself with happiness. She was not beautiful. She had been left completely disfigured by the accident: her eyes were unable to focus properly, one leg was longer than the other, and she walked with a limp. It was not those things that made her not beautiful, for the internal chaos her unfocused sight caused her could have led to an expression of vulnerability on her face; the limp, too, might have caused anyone to feel sympathetic toward her. But it was not so; she became more arrogant, she acquired a coarseness to her voice, her gaze became a hard stare, her figure grew wide and slow; she was not fury itself, only a woman disappointed with love when it comes through a man.

After they were married, they lived with her parents, a situation my father immediately, and correctly, guessed was a danger to me. Her husband did not love her, this she knew. He did not love me either; this she did not know. I called him Monsieur Pacquet, and this formality was meant to show a lack of interest, not to mention a lack of knowledge, in regard to him. He called me Mademoiselle; he could have called me Miss, but he liked the way the word passed through his lips, the flourish with which he said it. It was then that my father arranged for me to live with and work for his friend in Roseau, his friend the same doctor who had taken care of my sister when she was made an invalid and was lying in the hospital.

What makes the world turn?

Who would need an answer to such a question?

A man proud of the pale hue of his skin cherishes it especially because it is not a fulfillment of any aspiration, it is his not through any effort at all on his part; he was just born that way, he was blessed and chosen to be that way and it gives him a special privilege in the hierarchy of everything. This man sits on a plateau, not the level ground, and all he can see—fertile meadows, vast plains, high mountains with treasure buried deep within, turbulent seas, calm oceans—all this he knows with an iron certainty should be his own. What makes the world turn is a question he asks when all that he can see is securely in his grasp, so securely in his grasp that he can cease to look at it from time to time, he can denounce it, he can demand that it be taken away from him, he can curse the moment he was conceived and the day he was born, he can go to sleep at night and in the morning he will wake up and all he can see is still securely in his grasp; and he can ask again, What makes the world turn, and then he will have an answer and it will take up volumes and there are many answers, each of them different, and there are many men, each of them the same.

And what do I ask? What is the question I can ask? I own nothing, I am not a man.

I ask, What makes the world turn against me and all who look like me? I own nothing, I survey nothing, when I ask this question; the luxury of an answer that will fill volumes does not stretch out before me. When I ask this question, my voice is filled with despair.

There are seven days in a week, and why, I do not know. If I were to find myself in need of such things, days and weeks and months and years, it is not clear to me that I would arrange them the way I now find them. But all the same, here they are.

It was a Sunday in Roseau; the streets were disturbing, half-empty, quiet, clean; the water in the harbor was still, as if it were in a bottle, the houses were without the usual quarrelsome voices, the sky was a blue that was at once overwhelming and ordinary. The population of Roseau, that is, the ones who looked like me, had long ago been reduced to shadows; the forever foreign, the margins, had long ago lost any connection to wholeness, to an inner life of our own invention, and since it was a Sunday, some of them now were walking in a trance, no longer in their right minds, toward a church or away from a church. This activity—going to church, coming from church—had about it the atmosphere of a decree. It also signified defeat yet again, for what would the outcome have been of all the lives of the conquered if they had not come to believe in the gods of the people who had conquered them? I walked by a church. The church itself, a small beautiful structure, was meant to imitate in its simplicity and unworldliness a similar structure in a tiny village in some dark corner of England. But this church, typical of its time and place in every way, was built, inch by inch, by enslaved people, and many of the people who were slaves died while building this church, and their masters then had them buried in such a way that when the Day of Judgment came and all the dead were risen, the enslaved faces would not be turned toward the eternal light of heaven but toward the eternal darkness of hell. They, the slaves, were buried with their faces turned away from the east. But did the slaves have an interest in seeing eternal light in the first place, and what if the slaves preferred eternal darkness?

The pitiful thing is, an answer to these questions is no longer of use to anybody.

And so again, what makes the world turn? Most of the people inside that church would want to know. They were singing a hymn. The words were: "O Jesus, I have promised / To serve Thee to the end: / Be Thou for ever near me, / My Master and my friend." I wanted to knock on the church door then. I wanted to say, Let me in, let me in. I wanted to say, Let me tell you something: This Master and friend business, it is not possible; a master is one thing and a friend is something else altogether, something completely different; a master cannot be a friend. And who would want such a thing, master and friend at once? A man would want that. It is a man who would ask, What makes the world turn, and then would find in his own reply fields of gravity, imaginary lines, tilts and axes, reason and logic, and, quite brazenly, a theory of justice. And when he is done with that, he will say, Yes, but what really makes the world turn? and his mouth, grim with scorn for himself, will say the words: Connive, deceive, murder.

This man is not completely ignorant of the people inside the church, or those same people inside their small houses. His name is John or William, or something like that; he has a wife, her name is Jane or Charlotte, or something like that; he shoots plovers, he eats their eggs. His life is simple, he shuns excess because he wants to; or his life is an elaborate web of events, rituals, ceremonies because he wants it so. He is not ignorant of the many people in his thrall, this man; sometimes he likes the condition they are in and he would even die to keep them in it; sometimes he does not like the condition they are in and he would even die to remove them from it. He is not ignorant of them, he is not ignorant of them completely. They plant a field, they harvest its yield; he calculates with his sharp eye the fruits of their labor, which are tied up uniformly in bundles and lying on docks waiting to be shipped. This man makes a profit, sometimes larger than he expected, sometimes less than he expected. It is with this profit that the reality these many people represent is kept secret. For this man who says "My Master and my Friend" builds a large house, warms the rooms, sits in a chair made from a fabric that is very valuable because its origins are distant, obscure, and involve again the forced labor, the crippling, the early death of the unnamed many; sitting in this chair, he looks out a window; his forehead, his nose, his thin lips press against the glass; it is winter (something I will never see, a climate I will never know, and since I do not know it and since it holds nothing that is beautiful to me, I regard it with suspicion; I look down on people who are familiar with it but I, Xuela, am not in a position to do more than that). The grass is alive but not actively growing (dormant), the trees are alive but not actively growing (dormant); the hedge, its severely clipped shape a small monument to misery, separates two fields; the sun shines, but the light is pale and weak as if a great effort is being made. He is not looking at a graveyard; he is looking at a small part of all that he possesses, and the irregular mounds, gravelike in shape, caused by the earth first hardening, then softening then hardening again, already holding his ancestors and their deeds, have ample room for him and all that he will do and for all who come from him and all that they will do. His forehead, his nose, his thin lips are pressed ever harder against the window; in his mind the still earth becomes a blue sea, a gray ocean, and on the blue sea and on the gray ocean are ships, and the ships are filled with people, and the ships filled with people sink to the bottom of the blue sea and the gray ocean again and again. The blue sea and the gray ocean are also a small part of all he possesses, and they, with their surfaces smooth and tranquil, are a sign of covenants made, inviolable promises, but even so, the irregular mounds, gravelike in shape, appear, small swell swallowing up small swell, hiding a depth whose measure can be taken but the knowledge of it cannot overcome the fear. The impartiality of the dormant field outside his window is well known to him; it will accept a creature he finds a pest, it will accept his most revered ancestor, it will accept him; but the dormant field is carved up and it is spring (I am not familiar with this, I cannot find any joy in this, I think people associated with it are less than I am but I, Xuela, am not in a position to make my feeling have any meaning) and the field can be made to do something he wants it to do. The impartiality of the blue sea, the gray ocean, is well known to him also, but these cold, vast vaults of water cannot be carved up and no season can influence them in his favor; the blue sea, the gray ocean will take him along with all that represents his earthly happiness (the ship full of people) and all that represents his unhappiness (the ship full of people).

It is an afternoon in winter, the sky above him is a blue that is at once overwhelming and ordinary, there is a moon of pure white and not quite full in the middle of it. He is afraid. His name is John, he is the master of the people in the ship that sails on the blue sea, the gray ocean, but he is not master of the sea or the ocean itself. In his position as master, his needs are clear and paramount and so he is without mercy, he is without compassion, he is without tenderness. In his position as a man, unclothed, unfed, as a testament to ordinariness without his house with the warmed rooms, he meets the same fate as all he used to be master of; the ground outside his window will take him in; so will the blue sea, so will the gray ocean. And so it is that at the moment he finds himself in this position, the position of a man, an ordinary man, he asks that master be friend, he asks for himself the very thing that he cannot give; he asks and he asks, even though he knows such a thing is not possible; *such a thing is not possible*, but he cannot help himself, for always the first person you feel sorry for is your own self. And it is this person, this man, who says at a moment he needs to: God does not judge; and when he is saying this, God does not judge, he places himself in a childlike pose; his knees are crossed, his hands are clasped around them, and he will repeat to himself a parable, The Sower and the Wheat, and he gives it an interpretation favorable to himself: God's love shines equally on all the wheat wherever it may grow, between the rocks, in shallow ground, in good soil.

This short, bitter sermonette that I delivered to myself was not new to me. There was hardly a day of my life that I did not observe some incident to add fresh weight to this view, for to me history was not a large stage filled with commemoration, bands, cheers, ribbons, medals, the sound of fine glass clinking and raised high in the air; in other words, the sounds of victory. For me history was not only the past: it was the past and it was also the present. I did not mind my defeat, I only minded that it had to last so long; I did not see the future, and that is perhaps as it should be. Why should anyone see such a thing. And yet . . . and yet, it made me sad to know that I did not look straight ahead of me, I always looked back, sometimes I looked to the side, but mostly I looked back.

The church outside which I stood on that Sunday was very familiar to me, I had been baptized in it; my father had become such an outstanding member of it that he was now allowed to read the lesson during Sunday-morning service. As if obeying my summons, the congregation erupted from the church, and among them were my father, who no longer bore so much as a trace of the treachery he had committed by joining such a group of people, and Philip, the man I worked for but did not hate and who at the same time was a man I slept with but did not love and whom I would eventually marry but still not love. They were, this congregation, just then in a state of deep satisfaction, though they were not all in identical states of deep satisfaction; my father was less satisfied than Philip, his position in the group less secure. But my father was an incredible mimic and knew well how to make an ordinary person miserable and how to turn the merely miserable person into the person who cries out in the middle of the night, "What makes the world turn against me?" with a wail of anguish so familiar to the night itself, yet so strange to the person from whose being these words have made an involuntary escape. Just a glance not so far away would have provided a substantial example; at the far end of the cemetery, which abutted the churchyard, stood a man named Lazarus and he was making a hole in the ground, he was making a grave; the person to be buried in this grave so far away from the church would be a poor person, perhaps one of the merely miserable. I knew of Lazarus—his name would have been given to him in a moment of innocent hope; his mother would have thought that such a name, rich and powerful as it was with divine second chance, would somehow protect him from the living death that was his actual life; but it had been of no use, he was born the Dead and he would die the Dead. He was one of the many people with whom my father maintained a parasitic existence (even as the people with whom my father attended church maintained a parasitic existence with my father), and I knew of him because my mother was buried in this graveyard (I could not see her grave now from where I stood), and once when I was visiting it I came upon him face-to-face in the graveyard, carrying a bottle (pint size) of white rum in one hand and holding up the waist of his trousers with the other; an insect kept trying to feed from a small pool of saliva that had settled at the corner of his mouth, and he at first used the hand that held the bottle of rum to brush it away, but the insect persisted, and so, instinctively, without calculation, he let go of his pants waist and firmly brushed the insect away. The insect did go away, the insect did not return, but his trousers fell down to his ankles, and again instinctively, without calculation, he reached down to pull them back up and he became as he was before, a poor man driven out of his mind by a set of events that the guilty and the tired and the hopeless call life. He looked like an overworked beast, he looked like a living carcass; the bones in his body were too prominent, they were too close to his skin, he smelled sour, he smelled of stink, he smelled like something rotting, when it's in that sweet stage that can sometimes pass for a delicacy, just before real decay sets in; before his trousers met his waist again, I saw the only alive thing left of him; it was his pubic hair: it covered a large area of his crotch, growing in a wide circle, almost hiding all his private parts; its color was red, the red of a gift or the red of something burning rapidly. This brief meeting of a gravedigger and myself had no beginning and so it could have no end; there was only a "Good day" from me and an "Eh-eh" from him, and these things were said at exactly the same time, so that he did not really hear what

I said and I did not really hear what he said, and that was the point. The idea of him and me really hearing each other was out of the question; from the pain of it, we might have murdered ourselves or put in motion a chain of events that would have come to an end only with our hanging from the gallows at midday in a public square. He disappeared inside the Dead House, where he kept the tools of his trade: shovels, ladders, ropes.

The congregation stood on the church steps, basking in the heat, now strong, as if they knew with certainty that it held blessings, though only for them; they spoke to one another, they listened to one another, they smiled at one another; it was a pretty picture they made, like ants from the same nest; it was a pretty picture, for Lazarus was left out of it, I was left out of it. They bade each other goodbye and returned to their homes, where they would drink a cup of English tea, even though they were quite aware that no such thing as a tea tree grew in England, and later that night, before they went to bed, they would drink a cup of English cocoa, even though they were quite aware that no such thing as a cocoa tree grew in England.

At that time in my life, how did such a day come to an end? I was sitting on my bed without any clothes on, my legs over Philip's legs, and he also had no clothes on. He had just removed himself from inside me, and a warm saliva-like fluid leaked out of me, making a damp patch on the sheet. He was like most of the men I had known, obsessed with an activity he was not very good at, but he took directions very well and was not afraid of being told what to do, or ashamed that he did not know all the things there were to do. He had an obsessive interest in rearranging the landscape: not gardening in the way of necessity, the growing of food, but gardening in the way of luxury, the growing of flowering plants for no other reason than the pleasure of it and making these plants do exactly what he wanted them to do; and it made great sense that he would be drawn to this activity, for it is an act of conquest, benign though it may be. He had come into my room in his usual state: he said nothing, he showed nothing, he acted as if he were feeling nothing, and that suited me, for everyone I knew was so filled up with feelings and words, and often much of this was directed at impeding my will; but he had come into my room then holding a book, a book filled with pictures of ruins, not the kind that are the remains of a lost civilization, but purposely built decay. He was obsessed with this idea, too, decay, ruin, and that again made sense, for he came from people who had caused so much of it they might have eventually come to feel that they could not live without it. And pressed between the pages of this book were some specimens of flowers he had known and I suppose had loved, but flowers that could not grow in this Dominican climate; he would hold them up to the light and call out to me their names: peony, delphinium, foxglove, monkshood, and in his voice was at once the triumphant chord of the victor and the discordant melody of the dispossessed; for with this roll call of the herbaceous border (he had shown me a picture of such a thing, a mere grouping of some flowering plants) he would enter an almost etherlike induced trance and would recall everyday scenes from his childhood: what his mother did every Wednesday, the way his father trimmed his mustache, the smell of rainfall in the English countryside, puddings stiffened with eggs and not arrowroot; and how in summer his hair was freshly cut so that his head resembled the back of a baby animal and a swift evening breeze would cool off his hot scalp as he reached the top of some cliff after a day's walk over some moors; and the last sound he heard just before he fell asleep on the first night he spent away from his mother and father at school, and the friendliness of an English sky especially on Easter Sunday, and the *thwop* of a tennis ball—a white blur—punctuating the absolute stillness of an English summer afternoon; his mother standing in the shade of a tall beech, a basket filled with vegetables of distinction and character in one hand, a trowel in the other—on the whole, an outdoors full of natural, perfect symmetry, an indoors free of novelty, or the currently fashionable, and unpleasant smells.

And still without his exhibiting any excitement, the words would pour out of him, one on top of the other, like water rushing to a precipice, and I would grow tired of it, and it would cause me to take offense, and I would put a stop to it by removing my clothes and stand before him and stretch my arms all the way up to the ceiling and order him to his knees to eat and there make him stay until I was completely satisfied.

His face afterward was patterned with randomly placed fine lines, a set of shallow impressions made by the abundance of coarse hair that grew between my legs. He looked wonderfully human then, free of blame, not happy, only quite human. He used to be young, but he wasn't young anymore. He was about my father's age, about fifty, but it was not a surprise that he did not look it; my father had had to commit his own crimes against humanity: he wore on his face the number of people he had impoverished, the number of people to whose early death he had made a sizable contribution, the number of children he had fathered and then ignored, and so on; but by the time Philip was born, all the bad deeds had already been committed; he was an heir, generations of people had died and left him something. That this had not brought him eternal happiness, had not brought him earthly peace, would not save him from becoming familiar with the unknown, and might even have driven him to a corner of the world that he did not like, into the bed of a woman who did not love him, could not be doubted. He was a tall man, taller than my bed was long, and so he could not sleep in my bed. You could see in his hands that he had no confidence, no public confidence and none in private either: his hands were small, not in proportion to the rest of his body; they were pale, the color of a bad-luck cockroach in its pupa stage; they were not hands that could invent or gain a world, they were hands that could lose a world. I had been working for him as an assistant for over a year when because I could not get rid of a cough he had to listen to my chest. My breasts then were in a constant state of sensation, the breasts themselves small globes of reddish brown flesh, the nipples a fruit purple and pointed; they burned, they itched, and this sensation ceased only when a mouth, a man's mouth, was clamped tightly over them and sucking; I had long ago come to recognize this as perhaps an unremitting part of the way I really am and so I looked for a man who could offer relief from this sensation; I did not look for a husband, and so the sentences "I married him because he was so handsome," "I married him because I felt he was trustworthy," "I married him because I felt he would be a good provider" would never cross my lips. Because my breasts were in such a state, I wore strips of muslin wrapped tightly around my chest, as if to protect an old wound. To have Philip examine me I had to remove the bandage, and since he was a doctor I did this in his presence. I removed the muslin carefully, as if I were alone, and this was because I was in the presence of a doctor, not because I wanted him to find it interesting in any way. His voice had a strange quality, strange because it came from him, but familiar to me all the same; he sounded like a man, a very ordinary man, a man as I knew a man to be; it made me tell him exactly why I did that. I told him that my breasts were filled with an irritable sensation, an irritable sensation that I found pleasant because it could be relieved only by a sensation I found even more desirable, a man's mouth placed securely over them.

We were in the room where he examined patients, I was sitting on the table; the room had windows on three sides, the windows had adjustable wooden slats; the wooden slats were tilted half open and the sunlight came in through them, measured, each shaft three inches wide, and some of them fell halfway across the floor and ended there, and some of them fell diagonally across another part of the floor and then bent up against the wall and ended halfway there, and it gave the room a strange atmosphere, the pattern of shading and light, a fully clothed man, a woman explaining why she bandaged her breasts, a kerosene lamp on the shelf, a set of white enamel basins which held syringes and needles and forceps inside them on a mahogany table; and all of a sudden he must have felt excited, for he walked away from me and looked through one of the half-closed shutters, and of course he saw the end of the world, because the Roseau sky looked like that sometimes, it looked like heaven, the place to go when you don't want to think too much; and it's possible that he asked himself what he was doing in this part of the world, and it's possible that he remembered all the reasons that had brought him to this part of the world; any one of them would have made him sick. People say something was inevitable when they have a sense of helplessness, when something that seemed good turns out bad, and this for the millionth time; no one ever says this on his deathbed, the only time it is the appropriate thing to say, because nothing else is inevitable, not even the sun coming up in the morning, which you may not live to see.

What color was the night? Black. I was in my room. What time of night did he come to me? It was not too long after I heard the sound of the night guards' boots on the cobblestones; they were returning from their duty of guarding the governor's house, even though such a function, guarding the governor, was without any meaning whatsoever, because who would harm the governor? I would, I could easily cut off his head, but they would only send another governor, and even I would grow tired of this, cutting off his head. Did he knock at the door? Did I say, Come in? Did he open the door with some hesitation? Did he open the door quickly and come in with a mistaken look of being wanted on his face? Did he wipe his feet on the mat at the door? Did he close the door behind him? What color was his face? Was it pale and ghostly, cowardly, hollow, sad? Was it red, full of blood, excited, happy? Perhaps, perhaps. He wore a blue shirt, the shade of blue that the sea became at midday, and this surprised me, because I did not know that he would like such a color; he must have worn shoes; he must have just bathed, a scent came from him, a perfume for a man, a scent no man I had ever known could afford. He carried a book in his hand—he did that from the beginning—he carried it in his right hand and his index finger separated it into two parts. He said my name. My room was not too small, it was not too big; it was built to house his nurse, built to hold someone way above my social standing, someone way beneath his, someone who was not me, someone who was not him, someone who would keep me in my place, someone who would keep him in his; but no nurse ever came. I could feel the darkness of the night outside, a darkness no starlight could brighten, a darkness that discouraged movement unless you felt your feet had eyes; I could hear someone singing, a woman—it was an English woman; she was singing a sad song, a sad lullaby, but she herself was not sad, people who are sad do not sing at all. My room was lit by a small blue lamp whose base was made of porcelain with two flowers with multicolored petals painted on it—parrot tulips, Philip had told me they were called—and it gave off a light that made the room seem not romantic, not wicked, not warm, none of those things; it only gave light, not much light, because it was a small lamp; it had been my mother's lamp and would have been the last lamplight that she saw, because it was the lamp that lit the room at the time she died, which was the time I was born; and by this lamplight, too, she would have seen my father's face as he lay on top of her, just before he withdrew himself from inside her. But this small lamp gave not much light and Philip was carrying a book in his hand which he wanted to show to me, he thought; he really thought so, he thought he wanted to show it to me from the moment he picked it up from its place on a shelf just before he ate his dinner; and after his wife went to her bed and he stood in three doorways going in and out of rooms, and then he stepped out of his house and walked over to my room and was inside the door, and all the time he thought he wanted to show me this book, right up to the moment when I let him know I did not want to see it. I had been sitting on the floor caressing in an absentminded way various parts of my body. I was wearing a nightgown made from a piece of nankeen my father had given me, and when Philip came in, one hand was underneath it and my fingers were trapped in the hair between my legs. When he came in I did not remove my hand hurriedly. He said my name. I wanted to respond in a normal way, the way usually done when someone calls you. You say, "Yes?" and you wait for them to continue, but I could not do this, my voice felt as if it were trapped in my hand, the hand that was trapped in the hair between my legs. He then said nothing. The cuffs of his trousers rested on the top of his shoes; the trousers were made of linen and were a shade of beige that I did not like: long-dead bones are that color, empty shells are that color, it is one of the colors of decay, but a color he liked, many things he wore were this shade of beige; his shoes were brown, substantial, and shiny.

He was not at all the person I dreamed of lying on top of me, my legs wrapped around his waist; I was not without someone, I knew a man, a man I thought of in this way, a man I dreamed of, but he was not in that room with me right then, he was away, I did not know where, and until Philip came, I was alone in the room caressing myself, one of my hands purposely trapped in the hair between my legs. His hair was thin and yellow like an animal's that I was not familiar with; his skin was thin and pink and transparent, as if it were on its way to being skin but had not yet reached the state that real skin is; it was not the skin of anyone I have loved yet and not the skin I dreamed of; the veins showed through it here and there like threads sewn by a clumsy seamstress; his nose was narrow and thin like the small part of a funnel, and tilted up in the air as if on the alert for something, not like a nose I was used to being fond of. He did not look like anyone I could love, and he did not look like anyone I should love, and so I determined then that I could not love him and I determined that I should not love him. There is a certain way that life ought to be, an ideal way, a perfect way, and there is the way that life is, not quite the opposite of ideal, not quite the opposite of perfect, it just is not quite the way it should be but not quite the way it should not be either; I mean to say that in any situation, only one or two, maybe even three out of ten, things are just what you have been praying for. He called my name. He had placed the book he was carrying on a table, a table made of the wood taken from an oak tree, a table with three feet that ended in the shape of claws, a table that he had brought from England with him but had found no real use for and so it had been given to me or to whoever would occupy the room it was in. He called my name and it was as if he were imprisoned in the sound of my name; his voice was muffled, raspy, like someone not getting enough air, he was in despair, he was in tears, although no water came out of his eyes, he was not himself, he never would be in this room. I started to remove my nightgown, I pulled it over my head, I had plaited my hair into two braids and rolled them up along the side of my head, they covered my ears; the neck of my nightgown had too small an opening and so I stood before him, my arms above my head, my head inside my nightgown, naked. I do not know how long I stood like that, it could only have been a moment, but I became eternally fascinated with how I felt then. I felt a sensation between my legs that I was not unfamiliar with; he was not the first man I had been with, but I had not allowed myself to acknowledge how powerful a feeling it was, I myself had no word for it, I had never read a word for it, I had never heard someone else mention a word for it; the feeling was a sweet, hollow feeling, an empty space with a yearning to be filled, to be filled up until the yearning to be filled up was exhausted. He stood behind me and raced his tongue up and down the back of my neck. He helped me bring my nightgown back down over my body, and then he unraveled one plait of hair and I unraveled the other. He helped me remove my nightgown and it came off easily. Around his waist he wore a brown belt made of hemp dyed the same color brown as his shoes and I wanted to remove it, but I could not bear to see him naked, his skin in its almost skinness would remind me of the world, the world that was outside the room which was the dark night, the world that was beyond the dark night, and so I closed my eyes and I turned around and removed his belt, and using my mouth I secured it tightly around my wrists and I raised my hands in the air, and with my face turned sideways I placed my chest against a wall. I made him stand behind me, I made him lie on top of me, my face beneath his; I made him lie on top of me, my back beneath his chest; I made him lie in back of me and place his hand in my mouth and I bit his hand in a moment of confusion, a moment when

I could not tell if I was in agony or pleasure; I made him kiss my entire body, starting with my feet and ending with the top of my head. The darkness outside the room pressed against its four sides; inside, the room grew smaller and smaller as it filled up almost to bursting with hisses, gasps, moans, sighs, tears, bursts of laughter; but they had a deep twist to them, a spin, an edge, that transformed these sounds from their ordinary selves and would make you cover your ears unless they came from inside you, until you realized that they came from inside you; all these sounds came from me; he was silent then and he was always silent when he was in such a state; no words came from him, no sounds came from him, only sometimes he would murmur my name as if it held something, a meaning, a memory that perhaps he could not let go. He fell into a sleep, not the sleep of the contented, the sleep of the satisfied, but the sleep of the drunk; I did not mean peace to him (as he did not mean peace to me); I could not mean peace to him, it would have been dangerous for him if that had been so, the temptation to see him die I would have found overwhelming, I would not have been able to resist it.

His wife then was still alive, her name was Moira and she was still alive; they lived in the same house and ate the same meals together at the same time and did many things together, but they did not sleep in the same bed in the same room; they did many things together, went to church, saw the same people at the same time, but they did not sleep in the same bed in the same room, and though it made sense to me, for I, too, always choose to sleep, actually sleep, alone, I did not know how they came to such an arrangement and I did not know which of them required it. I did not know how they met, they did not look as if they could ever have been in love with each other, but even I did not trust that observation; after all, everybody is full of surprises. She was very pleased to be who she was, and by that she meant she was pleased to be of the English people, and that made sense, because it is among the first tools you need to transgress against another human being—to be very pleased with who you are. She liked her hair, it was black and cropped close to her head like a man's, and she would make a mixture of eggs, honey, and lemon juice and comb it through her hair to make it gleam. She liked her complexion and would not have described it in this way: waxy, ghostish, without life; she would have said of herself that she was kind, full of sympathy for others (she collected used clothes for victims of natural disasters), decent (she gave to the poor), full of grace, but in her present situation it did not matter and this situation was a climate she did not like, a place full of people she could never love. For days she would eat only fruit and complain that it was too sour or too sweet or the flesh not firm enough or the flesh too firm, and she would lie in the shade because the sun was too hot, or she would lie in a room with the windows shut to keep out the damp, or perhaps it was the darkness or something else. She wore only black or only gray or only white, and since she was very thin, bony, almost like something that used to be and had been long lost and then found, a remnant, fossil-like, these colors gave her a malicious quality; she looked like a vector, a vector of malaise, and then she would speak in long sentences, sentences that were hundreds of words long, and she would not pause for breath, and nothing was really said, just a strange sound in the air, an annoyance that was her voice, and my impulse to make it quiet with a swift blow had to be resisted. I did not like her and I should have liked her, or at least I should have had even a tiny bit of sympathy for her, because like me she also had a broken womb, but I could not tell if like me she had broken hers deliberately or if she was born that way. I did not like her; I did not like her, it was impossible, it was an impossible situation. We did not like ourselves, we did not like each other, and so it was impossible to like them; they had a quality of something other, something other than ourselves; we were human and they were not human, and each thing about them that was different from us made us doubt their reality; they were cruel in ways we had never thought of, they were one of the definitions of contradiction: they lived among people they did not like, they did not do this with ease, they did not do this in happiness, they did it anyway. Her otherness was not particularly offensive; it was just that I became more familiar with it. She sat in basins of cold water to make her hot body cool and then she sat in basins of hot water to make her cold body warm. When I saw her for the first time, she was standing in front of a mirror rubbing the small old stones that were her breasts, but with no aim to it as far as I could see: her mouth was not open, her legs were not spread slightly apart, her hands just moved back and forth in a circling motion around her breasts. Her eyes were a shade of blue more suited to a wide expanse like the sky or the sea, and set in her bone-dry face, they confirmed an ungenerous nature. I would always look forward to seeing her face, not with pleasure, from curiosity, and was always taken aback that it held nothing new: no softening, no tears, no regrets, no apology; she was a lady, I was a woman, and this distinction for her was important; it allowed her to believe that I would not associate the ordinary, the everyday—a bowel movement, a cry of ecstasy—with her, and a small act of cruelty was elevated to a rite of civilization. And so she would say, "There is a woman who holds shop every Tuesday at the corner of King George and Market Streets; tell her that the lady who bought . . ." It was an accurate description of herself, more so than she could have wanted it to be, for it is true that a lady is a combination of elaborate fabrications, a collection of externals, facial arrangements, and body parts, distortions, lies, and empty effort. I was a woman and as that I had a brief definition: two breasts, a small opening between my legs, one womb; it never varies and they are always in the same place. She would never describe herself in this way, she would shrink from such a description, such a description has at its core the act of self-possession, and at that moment my self was the only thing I had that was my own. It was not to her, then, that I could pose the question: Why do women hate each other? And this life that she (and Philip and all who looked like them) lived among us, this life of ease, this life of comfort, the result of a great triumph, a life that no one seems able to resist, dominion over others: it, too, was a life of death, a different death from the one of the gravedigger Lazarus, a different one from my own, but a death all the same, a living death, for each deed, good or bad, holds inside its self its own reward, good or bad; each act you commit is your gift to yourself. She died. I married her husband, but this is not to say that I took her place.

In the moments when Philip was inside me, in those moments when the pleasure of his thrusts and withdrawals waned and I was not a prisoner of the most primitive and most essential of emotions, that thing silently, secretly, shamefully called sex, my mind turned to another source of pleasure. He was a man that was Philip's opposite. His name was Roland.

His mouth was like an island in the sea that was his face; I am sure he had ears and nose and eyes and all the rest, but I could see only his mouth, which I knew could do all the things that a mouth usually does, such as eat food, purse in approval or disapproval, smile, twist in thought; inside were his teeth and behind them was his tongue. Why did I see him that way, how did I come to see him that way? It was a mystery to me that he had been alive all along and that I had not known of his existence and I was perfectly fine—I went to sleep at night and I could wake up in the morning and greet the day with indifference if it suited me, I could comb my hair and scratch myself and I was still perfectly fine—and he was alive, sometimes living in a house next to mine, sometimes living in a house far away, and his existence was ordinary and perfect and parallel to mine, but I did not know of it, even though sometimes he was close enough to me for me to notice that he smelled of cargo he had been unloading; he was a stevedore.

His mouth really did look like an island, lying in a twig-brown sea, stretching out from east to west, widest near the center, with tiny, sharp creases, its color a shade lighter than that of the twig-brown sea in which it lay, the place where the two lips met disappearing into the pinkest of pinks, and even though I must have held his mouth in mine a thousand times, it was always new to me. He must have smiled at me, though I don't really know, but I don't like to think that I would love someone who hadn't first smiled at me. It had been raining, a heavy downpour, and I took shelter under the gallery of a dry-goods store along with some other people. The rain was an inconvenience, for it was not necessary; there had already been too much of it, and it was no longer only outside, overflowing in the gutters, but inside also, roofs were leaking and then falling in. I was standing under the gallery and had sunk deep within myself, enjoying completely the despair I felt at being myself. I was wearing a dress; I had combed my hair that morning; I had washed myself that morning. I was looking at nothing in particular when I saw his mouth. He was speaking to someone else, but he was looking at me. The someone else he was speaking to was a woman. His mouth then was not like an island at rest in a sea but like a small patch of ground viewed from high above and set in motion by a force not readily seen.

When he saw me looking at him, he opened his mouth wider, and that must have been the smile. I saw then that he had a large gap between his two front teeth, which probably meant that he could not be trusted, but I did not care. My dress was damp, my shoes were wet, my hair was wet, my skin was cold, all around me were people standing in small amounts of water and mud, shivering, but I started to perspire from an effort I wasn't aware I was making; I started to perspire because I felt hot, and I started to perspire because I felt happy. I wore my hair then in two plaits and the ends of them rested just below my collarbone; all the moisture in my hair collected and ran down my two plaits, as if they were two gutters, and the water seeped through my dress just below the collarbone and continued to run down my chest, only stopping at the place where the tips of my breasts met the fabric, revealing, plain as a new print, my nipples. He was looking at me and talking to someone else, and his mouth grew wide and narrow, small and large, and I wanted him to notice me, but there was so much noise: all the people standing in the gallery, sheltering themselves from the strong rain, had something they wanted to say, something not about the weather (that was by now beyond comment) but about their lives, their disappointments most likely, for joy is so short-lived there isn't enough time to dwell on its occurrence. The noise, which started as a hum, grew to a loud din, and the loud din had an unpleasant taste of metal and vinegar, but I knew his mouth could take it away if only I could get to it; so I called out my own name, and I knew he heard me immediately, but he wouldn't stop speaking to the woman he was talking to, so I had to call out my name again and again until he stopped, and by that time my name was like a chain around him, as the sight of his mouth was like a chain around me. And when our eyes met, we laughed, because we were happy, but it was frightening, for that gaze asked everything: who would betray whom, who would be captive, who would be captor, who would give and who would take, what would I do. And when our eyes met and we laughed at the same time, I said, "I love you, I love you," and he said, "I know." He did not say it out of vanity, he did not say it out of conceit, he only said it because it was true.

His name was Roland. He was not a hero, he did not even have a country; he was from an island, a small island that was between a sea and an ocean, and a small island is not a country. And he did not have a history; he was a small event in somebody else's history, but he was a man. I could see him better than he could see himself, and that was because he was who he was and I was myself, but also because I was taller than he was. He was unpolished, but he carried himself as if he were precious. His hands were large and thick, and for no reason that I could see he would spread them out in front of him and they looked as if they were the missing parts from a powerful piece of machinery; his legs were straight from hip to knee, and then from the knee they bent at an angle as if he had been at sea too long or had never learned to walk properly to begin with. The hair on his legs was tightly curled as if the hairs were pieces of thread rolled between the thumb and the forefinger in preparation for sewing, and so was the hair on his arms, the hair in his underarms, and the hair on his chest; the hair in those places was black and grew sparsely; the hair on his head and the hair between his legs was black and tightly curled also, but it grew in such abundance that it was impossible for me to move my hands through it. Sitting, standing, walking, or lying down, he carried himself as if he was something precious, but not out of vanity, for it was true, he was something precious; yet when he was lying on top of me he looked down at me as if I were the only woman in the world, the only woman he had ever looked at in that way—but that was not true, a man only does that when it is not true. When he first lay on top of me I was so ashamed of how much pleasure I felt that I bit my bottom lip hard—but I did not bleed, not from biting my lip, not then. His skin was smooth and warm in places I had not kissed him; in the places I had kissed him his skin was cold and coarse, and the pores were open and raised.

Did the world become a beautiful place? The rainy season eventually went away, the sunny season came, and it was too hot; the riverbed grew dry, the mouth of the river became shallow, the heat eventually became as wearying as the rain, and I would have wished it away if I had not become occupied with this other sensation, a sensation I had no single word for. I could feel myself full of happiness, but it was a kind of happiness I had never experienced before, and my happiness would spill out of me and run all the way down a long, long road and then the road would come to an end and I would feel empty and sad, for what could come after this? How would it end?

Not everything has an end, even though the beginning changes. The first time we were in a bed together we were lying on a thin board that was covered with old cloth, and this small detail, evidence of our poverty—people in our position, a stevedore and a doctor's servant, could not afford a proper mattress—was a major contribution to my satisfaction, for it allowed me to brace myself and match him breath for breath. But how can it be that a man who can carry large sacks filled with sugar or bales of cotton on his back from dawn to dusk exhausts himself within five minutes inside a woman? I did not then and I do not now know the answer to that. He kissed me. He fell asleep. I bathed my face then between his legs; he smelled of curry and onions, for those were the things he had been unloading all day; other times when I bathed my face between his legs—for I did it often, I liked doing it—he would smell of sugar, or flour, or the large, cheap bolts of cotton from which he would steal a few yards to give me to make a dress.

What is the everyday? What is the ordinary? One day, as I was walking toward the government dispensary to collect some supplies—one of my duties as a servant to a man who was in love with me beyond anything he could help and so had long since stopped trying, a man I ignored except when I wanted him to please me—I met Roland's wife, face-to-face, for the first time. She stood in front of me like a sentry—stern, dignified, guarding the noble idea, if not noble ideal, that was her husband. She did not block the sun, it was shining on my right; on my left was a large black cloud; it was raining way in the distance; there was no rainbow on the horizon. We stood on the narrow strip of concrete that was the sidewalk. One section of a wooden fence that was supposed to shield a yard from passersby on the street bulged out and was broken, and a few tugs from any careless party would end its usefulness; in that yard a primrose bush bloomed unnaturally, its leaves too large, its flowers showy, and weeds were everywhere, they had prospered in all the wet. We were not alone. A man walked past us with a cutlass in his knapsack and a mistreated dog two steps behind him; a woman walked by with a large basket of food on her head; some children were walking home from school, and they were not walking together; a man was leaning out a window, spitting, he used snuff. I was wearing a pair of modestly high heels, red, not a color to wear to work in the middle of the day, but that was just the way I had been feeling, red with a passion, like that hibiscus that was growing under the window of the man who kept spitting from the snuff. And Roland's wife called me a whore, a slut, a pig, a snake, a viper, a rat, a lowlife, a parasite, and an evil woman. I could see that her mouth formed a familiar hug around these words—poor thing, she had been used to saying them. I was not surprised. I could not have loved Roland the way I did if he had not loved other women. And I was not surprised; I had noticed immediately the space between his teeth. I was not surprised that she knew about me; a man cannot keep a secret, a man always wants all the women he knows to know each other.

I believe I said this: "I love Roland; when he is with me I want him to love me; when he is not with me I think of him loving me. I do not love you. I love Roland." This is what I wanted to say, and this is what I believe I said. She slapped me across the face; her hand was wide and thick like an oar; she, too, was used to doing hard work. Her hand met the side of my face: my jawbone, the skin below my eye and under my chin, a small portion of my nose, the lobe of my ear. I was then a young woman in my early twenties, my skin was supple, smooth, the pores invisible to the naked eye. It was completely without bitterness that I thought as I looked at her face, a face I had so little interest in that it would tire me to describe it, Why is the state of marriage so desirable that all women are afraid to be caught outside it? And why does this woman, who has never seen me before, to whom I have never made any promise, to whom I owe nothing, hate me so much? She expected me to return her blow but, instead, I said, again completely without bitterness, "I consider it beneath me to fight over a man."

I was wearing a dress of light-blue Irish linen. I could not afford to buy such material, because it came from a real country, not a false country like mine; a shipment of this material in blue, in pink, in lime green, and in beige had come from Ireland, I suppose, and Roland had given me yards of each shade from the bolts. I was wearing my blue Irish-linen dress that day, and it was demure enough—a pleated skirt that ended quite beneath my knees, a belt at my waist, sleeves that buttoned at my wrists, a high neckline that covered my collarbone—but underneath my dress I wore absolutely nothing, no undergarments of any kind, only my stockings, given to me by Roland and taken from yet another shipment of dry goods, each one held up by two pieces of elastic that I had sewn together to make a garter. My declaration of what I considered beneath me must have enraged Roland's wife, for she grabbed my blue dress at the collar and gave it a huge tug, it rent in two from my neck to my waist. My breasts lay softly on my chest, like two small pieces of unrisen dough, unmoved by the anger of this woman; not so by the touch of her husband's mouth, for he would remove my dress, by first patiently undoing all the buttons and then pulling down the bodice, and then he would take one breast in his mouth, and it would grow to a size much bigger than his mouth could hold, and he would let it go and turn to the other one; the saliva evaporating from the skin on that breast was an altogether different sensation from the sensation of my other breast in his mouth, and I would divide myself in two, for I could not decide which sensation I wanted to take dominance over the other. For an hour he would kiss me in this way and then exhaust himself on top of me in five minutes. I loved him so. In the dark I couldn't see him clearly, only an outline, a solid shadow; when I saw him in the daytime he was fully dressed. His wife, as she rent my dress, a dress made of material she knew very well, for she had a dress made of the same material, told me his history: it was not a long one, it was not a sad one, no one had died in it, no land had been laid waste, no birthright had been stolen; she had a list, and it was full of names, but they were not the names of countries.

What was the color of her wedding day? When she first saw him was she overwhelmed with desire? The impulse to possess is alive in every heart, and some people choose vast plains, some people choose high mountains, some people choose wide seas, and some people choose husbands; I chose to possess myself. I resembled a tree, a tall tree with long, strong branches; I looked delicate, but any man I held in my arms knew that I was strong; my hair was long and thick and deeply waved naturally, and I wore it braided and pinned up, because when I wore it loose around my shoulders it caused excitement in other people—some of them men, some of them women, some of them it pleased, some of them it did not. The way I walked depended on who I thought would see me and what effect I wanted my walk to have on them. My face was beautiful, I found it so.

And yet I was standing before a woman who found herself unable to keep her life's booty in its protective sack, a woman whose voice no longer came from her throat but from deep within her stomach, a woman whose hatred was misplaced. I looked down at our feet, hers and mine, and I expected to see my short life flash before me; instead, I saw that her feet were without shoes. She did have a pair of shoes, though, which I had seen; they were white, they were plain, a round toe and flat laces, they took shoe polish well, she wore them only on Sundays and to church. I had many pairs of shoes, in colors meant to attract attention and dazzle the eye; they were uncomfortable, I wore them every day, I never went to church at all.

My strong arms reached around to caress Roland, who was lying on my back naked; I was naked also. I knew his wife's name, but I did not say it; he knew his wife's name, too, but he did not say it. I did not know the long list of names that were not countries that his wife had committed to memory. He himself did not know the long list of names; he had not committed this list to memory. This was not from deceit, and it was not from carelessness. He was someone so used to a large fortune that he took it for granted; he did not have a bankbook, he did not have a ledger, he had a fortune—but still he had not lost interest in acquiring more. Feeling my womb contract, I crossed the room, still naked; small drops of blood spilled from inside me, evidence of my refusal to accept his silent offering. And Roland looked at me, his face expressing confusion. Why did I not bear his children? He could feel the times that I was fertile, and yet each month blood flowed away from me, and each month I expressed confidence at its imminent arrival and departure, and always I was overjoyed at the accuracy of my prediction. When I saw him like that, on his face a look that was a mixture—confusion, dumbfoundedness, defeat—I felt much sorrow for him, for his life was reduced to a list of names that were not countries, and to the number of times he brought the monthly flow of blood to a halt; his life was reduced to women, some of them beautiful, wearing dresses made from yards of cloth he had surreptitiously removed from the bowels of the ships where he worked as a stevedore.

At that time I loved him beyond words; I loved him when he was standing in front of me and I loved him when he was out of my sight. I was still a young woman. No small impressions, the size of a child's forefinger, had yet appeared on the soft parts of my body; my legs were long and hard, as if they had been made to take me a long distance; my arms were long and strong, as if prepared for carrying heavy loads. I was in love with Roland. He was a man. But who was he really? He did not sail the seas, he did not cross the oceans, he only worked in the bottom of vessels that had done so; no mountains were named for him, no valleys, no nothing. But still he was a man, and he wanted something beyond ordinary satisfaction—beyond one wife, one love, and one room with walls made of mud and roof of cane leaves, beyond the small plot of land where the same trees bear the same fruit year following year—for it would all end only in death, for though no history yet written had embraced him, though he could not identify the small uprisings within himself, though he would deny the small uprisings within himself, a strange calm would sometimes come over him, a cold stillness, and since he could find no words for it, he was momentarily blinded with shame.

One night Roland and I were sitting on the steps of the jetty, our backs facing the small world we were from, the world of sharp, dangerous curves in the road, of steep mountains of recent volcanic formations covered in a green so humble no one had ever longed for them, of 365 small streams that would never meet up to form a majestic roar, of clouds that were nothing but large vessels holding endless days of water, of people who had never been regarded as people at all; we looked into the night, its blackness did not come as a surprise, a moon full of dead white light traveled across the surface of a glittering black sky; I was wearing a dress made from another piece of cloth he had given me, another piece of cloth taken from the bowels of a ship without permission, and there was a false pocket in the skirt, a pocket that did not have a bottom, and Roland placed his hand inside the pocket, reaching all the way down to touch inside me; I looked at his face, his mouth I could see and it stretched across his face like an island and like an island, too, it held secrets and was dangerous and could swallow things whole that were much larger than itself; I looked out toward the horizon, which I could not see but knew was there all the same, and this was also true of the end of my love for Roland.

My father's skin was the color of corruption: copper, gold, ore; his eyes were gray, his hair was red, his nose was long and narrow; his father was a Scots-man, his mother of the African people, and this distinction between "man" and "people" was an important distinction, for one of them came off the boat as part of a horde, already demonized, mind blank to everything but human suffering, each face the same as the one next to it; the other came off the boat of his own volition, seeking to fulfill a destiny, a vision of himself he carried in his mind's eye. It was a legal union and it took place in a Methodist church in the village of All Saints in the parish of St. Paul, Antigua, on a Sunday afternoon in the late nineteenth century. His name was John Richardson and her name was Mary; I do not know if the word "happiness" was associated with marriage then. They had two children, boys, named Alfred and Albert; Alfred became my father. What my father made of his parents I do not know. I do not know if his mother was beautiful; there was no picture of her and my father never spoke of her in that way. I do not know if his father was handsome; there was no picture of him and my father never spoke of him in that way. His mother would not have been born into slavery, but her parents most certainly would have been enslaved people; and so, too, his father then could not have been an owner of slaves but his parents might have been. How these two people met and fell in love then, I do not know; that they fell in love I do not know, but I do not rule it out, nor any other combination of feelings. This man named John Richardson was a trader of rum and he had lived all over the English-owned West Indies, longest in Anguilla, before he settled with his wife, Mary, in Antigua; he had many children with many different women in these places where he had lived, and they were all boys and they could tell that they were the sons of John Richardson because they all had the same red hair, a red hair of such uniqueness that they were all proud to have it, the hair of John Richardson. This I knew because my father would tell people that he was a son of this man and he would describe his father in this way, as a man who had lived in this place and that place and had children, all of them boys with red hair, and that whenever he himself saw a man with red hair he would know that this man was related to him and he would always say these things with pleasure and with pride and not with irony or bitterness or sadness at the trail of misery this drunk from Scotland would have left in his wake.

I did not have red hair, I was not a man.

His mother remained to him without clear features, though she must have mended his clothes, cooked his food, tended his schoolboy wounds, encouraged his ambitions, soothed his wounded brow; these are things I would have liked my mother to have done, if only I had had one. John Richardson was eventually lost in a squall at sea, a convenient event, for I would not be surprised to learn that he had after all returned to Scotland, where he had more children, all of them boys with red hair of a different texture. Mary died of something not very long after, perhaps of heartbreak, perhaps not. My father did not attend her funeral, he was then a policeman in St. Kitts and already on his way to establishing his own small dynasty of red-haired boys; he did not marry yet. He was tall, and by a standard that was not my own, he was thought to be very handsome; all the clothes he wore were becoming to him; he looked very good in his uniform, he looked very good in the linen suit he wore to church on Sundays; he was a vain man, so vain that he had trained himself not to steal glances at his own reflection in public; I believe he spent much time in a room with the door locked rehearsing various poses he would take up in public, while leading his family to think he was preparing a lesson for Sunday school; he was an ambitious man, he liked to do things well and he did not like his effort to go unrecognized. He never carried money in his pocket, he would never surround himself with actual money, but this was not unlike training himself not to glance at his own reflection in public: to be seen with money was to reveal how much he loved it, and he loved a farthing more than he loved a penny and he loved a penny more than he loved a shilling and he loved a shilling more than he loved a pound, and this would seem crazy only to a person who doesn't understand money or love, a person like myself; but my father, who did not understand love when it applied to a person, only love when it came to money, understood that it was in the small parts of something that its true whole is expressed, it is in the small parts of something that its real beauty lies. He knew that there were 960 farthings in one pound and that 960 farthings scattered across the floor of an empty room are mesmerizing, enchanting, and seen by the right person are the foundation on which worlds are built. He was cruel especially to children and people in a weaker position than himself; he was not a coward, it is only that he never really felt rage at anybody more powerful than himself. He seemed to regard his life, himself, all of his surroundings, with humor; he wore a smile on his lips at all times when he was in public, but it was directed inward, not outward; this smile also served another purpose and perhaps he had not intended it to: it made people less powerful than he hesitate to approach him and it made people more powerful than he comfortable approaching him; and yet again the smile was a disguise, something he made himself do in public; he made himself smile with the same determination he made himself not glance at his own reflection; it was to mask all that he felt toward his fellow men, and all that he felt was not good. I never grew to like my father; perhaps I loved him, but I could not bring myself to admit it. I did not like him. Inside my father, the Scots-man and the African people met; I do not know how he felt about that; I do not know if that was one of the things he thought of when he sat in a room in his house, a room that had a view of the sea, the black Dominica sea, a sea that was a tomb, and his history which was made up of man and people was locked up in it. Such a position could have left him paralyzed as to which to be, man or people; his complexion, which was the color of corruption: gold, copper, ore (though if I had loved him, had felt sympathetic to him, I would have described it as the color of bread, the staff of life), made him look more like the victor (the Scots-man) than the vanquished (the African people), but that was not the reason to choose the one over the other. My father rejected the complications of the vanquished; he chose the ease of the victor. In the vanquished, had he looked, he could have felt the blankness that all human beings are confronted with day after day, a blankness that they hope to fill and sometimes succeed in filling, but then again, mostly not; and these people, these African people in whom he could have found one half of himself—they, too, being human, would have felt the blankness and they would have tried to fill it with the usual things: time divided into years, months, days, or something like that. They, too, would have made a fetish of the ordinary: the outer skin of the penis, the thin membrane at the opening of the vagina; they, too, would have made things, utensils from a variety of materials, in a variety of shapes, for a variety of uses; they, too, would have observed some violent occurrence in nature—the earth rupturing, seas where dry land used to be, darkness where light used to be—and would have found in these occurrences promises of some kind, ways to live by, rituals, and a sense of specialness, for they had been spared; and they, too, would have had myths of beginnings and myths of ends. The blankness is the chaos from which they had rescued themselves and given their life order, from there to there and back again, and in just this way. And it was from this life that those people were taken away by the Scots-man or some other hyphenated man who cannot exist as just a man but only with a hyphen.

Outside, outside my father, outside the island on which he was born, outside the island on which he now lived his life, the world went on in its way, each event large, a rehearsal for the future, each event large, a recapitulation of the past; but inside, inside my father (and also inside the island on which he was born, inside the island on which he now lived), an event that occurred hundreds of years before, the meeting of man and people, continued on a course so subtle that it became a true expression of his personality, it became who he really was; and he came to despise all who behaved like the African people: not all who looked like them, only all who behaved like them, all who were defeated, doomed, conquered, poor, diseased, head bowed down, mind numbed from cruelty. And he believed he was being himself one day when a man named Lazarus, a gravedigger, came to ask him for some nails to help rebuild the roof of his house; his house had been a dainty little structure of pine painted red and yellow and it had been destroyed in a hurricane two years before; my father was the highest government official in Mahaut then, he was given by the colonial government various things to give for free to people in the most need whenever there was a disaster; in the case of the hurricane he was given building materials of a not very good quality. My father did dispose of some of the things in the proper way, giving them to people in need, but just enough not to cause a scandal; the rest he sold, and the more a person was unable to pay, the more they were in need, the more he charged them. Lazarus was such a person, more unable to pay and more in need; in him, too, the event of the African people meeting the hyphenated man had taken on such subtlety that any way he chose to express himself was only a reminder of this: a happy song for him would be all about the idea of freedom, not a day spent lying on the sand near the sea in aimless pleasure. And so when Lazarus asked my father for the nails to complete the roof on his house, within my father the struggle between the hyphenated man and the horde had long since been resolved, the hyphenated man as before had triumphed, and my father told Lazarus that he did not have any nails left. I was ten years old at that time; I did not know my mother, she had died at the moment I came out of her, I knew only my father. I did not understand him; I loved to look at him from a short distance where he could not see me looking at him, his red hair glinting in the sun; I loved to look at him when he wore his dress uniform of navy-blue serge pants and white cotton twill jacket with gold buttons, the uniform he wore to a parade celebrating the English king's birthday. But at that moment when he denied Lazarus the nails, he started to become real, not just my father, but who he might really be. I knew that he had a large barrel of nails and other things in a shed at the back of the house, so in innocence, believing that he might have completely forgotten about it, I reminded him of it, I told him of the barrel full of nails, I told him just where the barrel was, what the barrel looked like, what the nails looked like, what the nails lying in the barrel one on top of the other—frozen, shiny—looked like. He denied again that he had any nails at all. The sound of his voice was not new; it was just that I heard him for the first time. It did not cause anything inside me to shatter, it did not cause anything outside me to shatter, it was not sudden, it was not unexpected, though I was not expecting it either—it was natural, an accepted fact, like the unevenness of height to be found in mountains, or the blue of a sky, or the moon. This was my father, the man I had always known, only there was more of him.

After Lazarus left, without the nails he had come for, without the nails he needed, my father grabbed me by the back of the neck of the dress I was wearing and dragged me through the house to the shed where he had the barrel of nails, and he pushed me facedown into the barrel of nails, at the same time saying in French patois, "Now you know where the nails are, now you really know where the nails are." He spoke patois, French or English, only with his family or with anyone who knew him from the time he was a boy, and I associated him speaking patois with expressions of his real self and so I knew that this pain he was causing me, this suffocating me in a barrel of nails, was a true feeling of his. He gave my head one last push and then he quickly left me. He went to sit in the room that looked out on the sea, the room that had no real purpose, it was used so infrequently; the sea's surface was still, and as he looked at it he removed wax from his ear and ate it.

And what could my father have been thinking as he sat in that room, as he sat on a chair which was a copy of a chair seen in a painting of some dreadful Englishman's drawing room, a chair copied by the hands of someone of whom he had no doubt taken advantage? What could he have been thinking as he looked at that sea, its surface sometimes heaving, its surface sometimes still? A human being, a person, many people, a people, will say that their surroundings, their physical surroundings, form their consciousness, their very being; they will get up every morning and look at green hills, white cliffs, silver mountains, fields of golden grain, rivers of blue-glinting water, and in the beauty of this—and it is beautiful, they cannot help but find it beautiful—they invisibly, magically, conquer the distance that is between them and the beauty they are beholding, and they feel themselves become one with it, they draw strength from it, they are inspired by it to sing songs, to compose verse; they invent themselves and reinvent themselves and they are inspired (again), but this time to commit small actions, small deeds, and eventually large actions, large deeds, and each success brings a validation of the original idea, the original feeling, the meeting of people and place, you and the place you are from are not a chance encounter; it is something beyond destiny, it is something so meant to be that it is beyond words. For my father, the sea, the big and beautiful sea, sometimes a shimmering sheet of blue, sometimes a shimmering sheet of black, sometimes a shimmering sheet of gray, could hold no such largesse of inspiration, could hold no such abundance of comfort, could hold no such anything of any good; its beauty was lost to him, blank; to look at it, to see it, was to be reminded of the despair of the victor and the despair of the vanquished at once; for the emptiness of conquest is not lost on the conqueror, faced as such a person is with the unending desire for more and more and more, until only death silences this desire; and the bottomless well of pain and misery that the conquered experiences—no amount of revenge can satiate or erase the perpetration of a great injustice. And so as in my father there existed at once victor and vanquished, perpetrator and victim, he chose, not at all surprisingly, the mantle of the former, always the former; this is not to say that he was at war with himself; this is only to say that he proved himself commonly human, for except for the saints who among us would not choose to be among the people with head held up, not head bowed down, and even the saints know that in the end of ends they will be among the ones with heads held up.

The callous, the cynical, the unbeliever will say, perhaps in a moment free of gravity, perhaps in a moment when they see in a blinding flash the world end and refuse to begin again, that life is a game: a game that the better of them wins, a game that the worse of them loses: a game in which to win is to gain everything and to lose is to get nothing, or a game of musical chairs in which, when the music stops, to win is to sit down and never make room for the loser, who is doomed to stand up forever. It goes without saying that to be among the callous, the cynical, the unbelievers, is to be among the winners, for those who have lost are never hardened to their loss; they feel it deeply, always, into eternity. No one who has lost dares to doubt, really doubt, human goodness; for the one who has lost, the last breath is a sigh, "Oh God." Always.

It was not without understanding, it was not without some pity, that I observed my father. When he was a boy—an idea, a reality I sometimes found hard to grasp: him soft, in need of warmth or soothings from rampaging fevers, bruised knees and elbows, in need of reassurance as his boy-strong will would weaken and falter, in need of other reassurance: the sun will come up again, the tide will go out, the rain will stop, the earth's turning cannot be stilled (I could only believe in this reality blindly, since such a state would not be unusual, but he had built so completely another skin over his real skin, a skin invisible to the eye but as real all the same as the protective shell of a turtle or the shield of a warrior)—when my father was a boy, he was given an egg by a neighbor of his mother and father. It was a thank-you gift from this woman because my father had been very kind to her—she was old and lived alone and he ran errands for her sometimes without being asked and never expected to be thanked—and when she gave him the egg—she had three hens, a cock, and a pig, they lived in her yard near the latrine, the fowls slept in a tree that rose up above it—he was surprised, he had never expected to be thanked at all, and he took this egg—it was brown with darker brown speckles all over it—and did not make an omelette or any other kind of meal with it but placed it under a hen, another hen which belonged to his mother, to set along with some other eggs, and when they were all hatched, he claimed one of the chickens as his own. That chicken became a hen and laid eggs and those eggs were set and became chickens and those chickens laid eggs and so on, an endless cycle interrupted only by the sale of some eggs and some chickens, and with the farthings, halfpennies, and pennies that they brought in exchange and profit. He never ate eggs after that (not all the time I knew him); he never ate chickens after that (not all the time I knew him), only collecting the bright red copper of money and polishing it so that it shone and giving it to his mother, who placed it in an old sock and kept it in her bosom awake and asleep. When his father was returning to Scotland for a visit on his journey, which was said to have ended with drownings at sea, my father gave his father the profit that had started with that original egg: a gift; it had grown into an enormous amount, enough to purchase material,

English material, to make a suit for wearing only on Sundays. But my father never saw his father again, my father never saw his profit again, and he may have spent the rest of his life trying to find and fit into that first suit he had imagined himself in again and again—though he would not have known he was doing that, I believe—and his whole life may have been a succession of rewards he could never enjoy, though he would not have seen that.

"It was a beautiful day, a day of such beauty that it remains stamped forever on my memory," my father would say to me, telling me of the day his father boarded a boat that sailed to Scotland; it never reached its destination, and so this picture that began in sunshine ended in the black of cold water, and my father's face, my father's very being, was the canvas on which it was painted. I was a small girl, eight years old, when he first began to tell me about this important detail in his life, the same age he was when he learned he would never see his father again. I was not physically robust, my voice was weak, I was female, I spoke to him only in English, proper English. He sat in a chair made of a wood found in India, and the arms of this chair, too, ended in the form of the closed paw of an animal whose name I did not know, and so did its two front legs, and I sat across from him on a floor that had been polished the day before and held in a tight grip the skirt of the white poplin dress I was wearing, and the poplin itself was from somewhere far away from here, the room in which we sat was the room that served no particular purpose. His face, as he spoke of the last time he saw his father, became a series of geometric references, regular and irregular lines, sharp and soft angles, the shallow surfaces beneath his cheeks growing full and round; he looked like the boy he had been then, or certainly the boy he thought he had been then, and his voice became liquid and soft, golden, as if he were speaking of someone else, not himself, someone he used to know very well, not himself, and had loved deeply, still not himself. His father sailed on a ship called the *John Hawkins*, but the name of that infamous criminal was not what caused my father's face to darken, soiled, criminal, that was not what made the light go out in his small boy's eyes.

Did my father ever say to himself, "Who am I, who am I?" not as a cry coming from the dark hole of despair but as a sign that from time to time he was inflicted with the innocent curiosity of the foolish? I do not know; I cannot know. Did he know himself? If the answer is yes, or if the answer is yes but not completely, or if the answer is yes but in an extremely narrow way, he would have had secret pleasures equal to the measure in which he knew himself; but I do not know, I do not know the answer. I did not know him, he was my father but I did not know him; everything I say about him is only my observation, only my opinion, and this must be a point of shame for all children—it was for me—that this person who was one of the two sources of my own existence was unknown to me, not a mystery, just not known to me.

When my father first ran his hand over my mother's skin—the skin on her face, the skin on her legs, the skin between her legs, the skin on her arms, the skin underneath her arms, the skin on her back, the skin below her back, the skin on her breasts, the skin below her breasts—he would not have likened its texture to satin or silk, for no extraordinary preciousness and beauty had been assigned to her; the color of her skin—brown, the deep orange of an old sunset—was not the result of a fateful meeting between conqueror and vanquished, sorrow and despair, vanity and humiliation; it was only itself, an untroubled fact: she was of the Carib people. He would not have asked, Who are the Carib people? or, more accurately, Who *were* the Carib people? for they were no more, they were extinct, a few hundred of them still living, my mother had been one of them, they were the last survivors. They were like living fossils, they belonged in a museum, on a shelf, enclosed in a glass case. That these people, my mother's people, were balanced precariously on the ledge of eternity, waiting to be swallowed up in the great yawn of nothingness, was without doubt, but the most bitter part was that it was through no fault of their own that they had lost, and lost in the most extreme way; they had lost not just the right to be themselves, they had lost themselves. This was my mother. She was tall (I am told—I did not know her, she died at the moment I was born); her hair was black, her fingers were long, her legs were long, her feet were long and narrow with a high instep, her face was thin and bony, her chin was narrow, her cheekbones high and wide, her lips were thin and wide, her body was thin and long; she had a natural graceful gait; she did not speak much. She perhaps never said anything that was very important, no one has ever told me; I do not know what language she spoke; if she ever told my father that she loved him, I do not know in what language she would have said such a thing. I did not know her; she died at the moment I was born. I never saw her face, and even when she appeared to me in a dream I never saw it, I saw only the back of her feet, her heels, as she came down a ladder, her bare feet, coming down, and always I woke up before I could see her going up again.

When my mother was born (so I was told) her

mother wrapped her in some clean pieces of cloth and placed her outside a place where some nuns from France lived; they brought her up, baptized her a Christian, and demanded that she be a quiet, shy, long-suffering, unquestioning, modest, wishing-to-die-soon person. She became such a person. The attachment, spiritual and physical, that a mother is said to have for her child, that confusion of who is who, flesh and flesh, that inseparableness which is said to exist between mother and child—all this was absent between my mother and her own mother. How to explain this abandonment, what child can understand it? That attachment, physical and spiritual, that confusion of who is who, flesh and flesh, which was absent between my mother and her mother was also absent between my mother and myself, for she died at the moment I was born, and though I can sensibly say to myself such a thing cannot be helped—for who can help dying—again how can any child understand such a thing, so profound an abandonment? I have refused to bear any children.

And what could her actual life as a child with such people have been like—for there could not have been any joy in it, no moment of pure leisure in which she would have been an imaginary queen of an imaginary country with an imaginary army to conquer imaginary people, such a thing being the sole property of a mind free of the coarseness of living, as a child's mind should be. She wore a dress made of nankeen, a loose-fitting dress, a shroud; it covered her arms, her knees, it fell all the way down to her ankles. She wore a matching piece of cloth on her head that covered all of her beautiful hair completely.

When did my father first see her? It is possible that he first saw her on a clear yet misty Dominica morning (such a thing does exist) coming toward him on the narrow path that winds its way (the road) around the perimeter of the island (a large mass jutting out of the larger sea), a bundle on the top of her head, and no doubt to him her beauty would have lain not in the structure of her face, the litheness of her figure (I do not know, I can only imagine this), an intelligence that he could sense from the expression on her face; no, it would have lain in her sadness, her weakness, her long-lost-ness, the crumbling of ancestral lines, her dejectedness, the false humility that was really defeat. He at that time was no longer just an ordinary, low, coarse henchman; by then he wore a uniform and it might have even had a ribbon or a marking of some kind to show that he had been properly cruel and unkind to people who did not deserve it. He had by then been from island to island and fathered children with women whose names he did not remember, the children's names he did not know at all. He must have felt when he saw her the need to stay in one place. My poor mother! Yet to say it makes me feel sad not to have known her would not be true at all; I am only sad to know that such a life had to exist. Each day the question whether to live or die, which should it be, must have stood before her. A courtship of this woman would not have taxed his imagination. They were married in a church in Roseau and within a year she was buried in its churchyard. People say he suffered over this loss, the loss of the only woman he had married; people say he was broken by this; people say he did not enjoy life then; people say that a great sadness came over him and this led to a deep devotion to God and he became a deacon in his church. People say this, people say these things, but people cannot say that because of his own suffering he identified with and had sympathy for the sufferings of others; people cannot say that his loss made him generous, kindhearted, unwilling always to take advantage of others, that goodness in him grew and grew, completely overshadowing his faults, his defects; people cannot say these things, because they would not be true.

And this woman whose face I have never seen, not even in a dream—what did she think, what thoughts crossed her mind when she first saw this man? It is possible that he appeared as yet another irresistible force, the last in her life; it is possible that she loved him passionately.

It is sad that unless you are born a god, your life, from its very beginning, is a mystery to you. You are conceived; you are born: these things are true, how could they not be, but you don't know them; you only have to believe them, for there is no other explanation. You are a child and you find the world big and round and you have to find a place in it. How to do that is yet another mystery, and no one can tell you how exactly. You become a woman, a grown-up person. Against ample evidence, against your better judgment, you put trust in the constancy of things, you place faith in their everydayness. One day you open your door, you step out in your yard, but the ground is not there and you fall into a hole that has no bottom and no sides and no color. The mystery of the hole in the ground gives way to the mystery of your fall; just when you get used to falling and falling forever, you stop; and that stopping is yet another mystery, for why did you stop, there is not an answer to that any more than there is an answer to why you fell in the first place. Who you are is a mystery no one can answer, not even you. And why not, why not!

The present is always perfect. No matter how happy I had been in the past I do not long for it. The present is always the moment for which I live. The future I never long for, it will come or it will not; one day it will not. But it does not loom up before me, I am never in a state of anticipation. The future is not even like the black space above the sky, with an intermittent spark of light; it is more like a room with no ceiling or floor or walls, it is the present that gives it such a shape, it is the present that encloses it. The past is a room full of baggage and rubbish and sometimes things that are of use, but if they are of real use, I have kept them.

I married a man I did not love, but I would not have married a man I loved at all. I married my father's friend, a man named Philip Bailey, a man trained to heal the sick, and in this he would succeed from time to time, but even so, only temporarily, for everyone, everywhere, succumbs eventually to the overwhelming stillness that is death. He loved me and then after that he longed for me and then after that he died. He died a lonely man, far away from the place where he was born, far away from all that had sustained him as a child, away from a woman who might have loved him, his first wife. She had died when he married me. His friends abandoned him, for they realized that his feelings for me were genuine, and he loved me. They did not attend our wedding. After we were married we moved far away into the mountains, into the land where my mother and the people she was of were born.

By the time I had married, my own womb had dried up, shriveled like an old piece of vegetable matter left out too long. The other parts of my body were drying up also; my skin did not so much wrinkle as the moisture in it seemed to evaporate. I had never ceased to observe myself, and at the time I could see that what I had lost in physical appeal or beauty I had gained in character. It was written all over me; I did not fail to arouse curiosity in anyone capable of it. I had been talked about, I had been judged and condemned. I had been loved and I had been hated. I now stood above it all, it all lay at my feet. It was said of me that I had poisoned my husband's first wife, but I had not; I only stood by and watched her poison herself every day and did not try to stop her. She had discovered—I had introduced the discovery to her—that the large white flowers of a most beautiful weed, when dried and brewed into a tea, created a feeling of well-being and induced pleasant hallucinations. I had become acquainted with this plant through one of my many wanderings while freeing my womb from burdens I did not want it to bear, burdens I did not want to bear, burdens that were a consequence of pleasure, not a consequence of truth; but this plant was not otherwise useful to me because I was not in need of a feeling of well-being, I was not in need of pleasant hallucinations. Eventually her need for this tea grew stronger and stronger, and it turned her skin black before she died. She had lived among people whose skin was such a color for most of her life, and for that very reason and that reason only she had despised them; she knew nothing of them, except that the protective covering of their shell, their skin, was the color black, and she did not like it, but this was the color she became before she died, black, and perhaps she liked it and perhaps she didn't, but all the same, she died anyway. I was often touched by her suffering, for she did suffer, and then again, often I was not. Before she fell into her final reverie, she demanded and she demanded, and all her demands were based on who she thought she was, and who she thought she was was based on her country of origin, which was England. The complications of who she thought her very self to be were lost on her; she was not unlike my own sister Elizabeth. My husband's wife, this fragile human being, drew her sense of who she was from the power of her country of origin, a country which at her time of birth had the ability to determine the everyday existence of one quarter of the world's human population, and in her small mind, she believed this situation to be not only a destiny but eternal, without any awareness of the limitations of her own self or any sympathy for her own fragility. She thought of herself as someone with values and manners and a strong certainty of the world, as if there could be nothing new, as if things had come to a standstill, as if with the arrival of her and her kind, life had reached such perfection that everything else, everything that was different from her, should just lie down and die. It was she who would lie down and die; everything else went on and it, too, eventually would lie down and die, but something more indescribable than vanity, something beyond fear, perhaps it was ignorance, made her believe that the world as she knew it was perfect. But she died and turned to dust, or dirt, or the wind, or the sea, or whatever it is we all turn into when we die.

My father died also, not so very long after I married his friend. What made them friends? My father admired Philip's garden, in which he grew fruit from the various tropical regions of the world, only he forced them to become a size they were not normally; sometimes he made them grow larger, sometimes he made them mere miniatures. Philip belonged to that restless people unable to leave the world alone, unable to look at anything for too long without becoming troubled by its very existence; silence is alien to them. My father, too, was of a restless mind, but fate, the act of conquest, had made him stay put. He could only look at this man Philip and watch him grow a mango the size of an adult's head, but then the fruit had no taste, it was only beautiful to look at; he then devoted much time to making this food pleasing to the taste buds. I never knew if Philip succeeded; I never ate any of the things he grew.

My father took a long time to die. He suffered much pain and his suffering almost made me believe in justice, but only almost, for there are many wrongs that nothing can ever make right, the past in the world as I know it is irreversible. He did not mind dying, he said. He spoke very movingly about the world of dying and the world of death, and he spoke very movingly of the life he had led. I did not recognize the life he had led when he spoke of it; I also was not moved. His life, of course, looked splendid to him; if it had not, he would have forgiven himself through a show of repentance, a display of good works. All the people he had robbed of their worldly goods were dead or nearly so; all the people who had robbed him of his worldly goods, who had defeated any effort he might have made to be a human being, were dead or would eventually be so. Still, as he lay dying, he could see the enormous amount of land he had acquired, each square of rich volcanic soil covered with some valuable crop: coffee, vanilla, grapefruit trees, lime trees, lemon trees, bananas. He owned many houses in Roseau, and at the end of each month, a half-dead man—for my father near the end of his life had his own henchmen and underlings who worked for him—brought him the rent that had been collected from tenants who sometimes had not much to eat. He died a rich man and did not believe that this would prevent him from entering the gates of the place he called heaven.

I missed him when he died, and before he died I knew this would be so. I wished not to miss him, but all the same it was so. I had never known my mother and yet my love for her followed her into eternity. My mother had died when I was born, unable to protect herself in a world cruel beyond ordinary imagining, unable to protect me. My father was able to protect me; but he did not. I believe instead that at an early age he placed me in the jaws of death. How I escaped I cannot fathom to answer myself. I did not love my father, I grew to love not loving my father, and I missed his presence, the irritant that was this loveless love. He died. I saw the light go out of his eyes, I saw the breath leave his body, I felt his skin turn from warm to cold. For a long time, hours after he was dead, he looked the way he had when he was alive, just there, still, and then he looked like something else, anything else, everything else when it is dead. He was stilled; his body was stilled, his mind was stilled. It was at that moment that I knew death to be a real thing; my mother's death in comparison was not a death at all.

I chose the clothes my father was buried in; they were the clothes he wore to my sister's wedding, a white suit made of Irish linen. I was allowed to do this, to choose his clothes, since his wife had long ago lost interest in him. My sister ceded this honor to me because of the superior position in which my marriage had placed me: Philip was of the conquering class. She was in awe of this, my own conquest—this was how she viewed it—and she despised me even more for it. That Philip was empty of real life and energy, used up, too tired even to give himself pleasure, that I did not love him, never occurred to her; it never occurred to her that my marriage represented a kind of tragedy, a kind of defeat, nothing, though, that would make the world hesitate to spin—none of this occurred to her.

For many hours after he was dead, my father looked the same; his features were the same as they had been when I knew him: he had a faint smile on his face, his lips were stretched open slightly, his closed eyes were almost lost in the folds of skin above his cheeks, his large ears stood up away from his head, awkwardly if you did not like the way they looked, beautifully if they pleased you. I loved my father's ears. His skin then, just after he had died, looked like the color of something useful: cooking utensils, copra, the earth, the color of the day early in the morning when it is no longer dark but not yet light. Within hours of the last breath leaving his body, he looked like the dead: anonymous, without character, without individuality. If you had not known him, you could not tell if his life had been distinguished by deeds good or bad, deeds of any kind at all. He looked like the dead, he could not say his name, he could not give an account of himself, he could not defend himself; he was of that world, the world of the dead, a world beyond silence; nothing. When I looked down at him, I felt a great sadness. I felt such pity, for he was dead; he would never walk again, he would never speak again. All the things that had pleased him, the fruits of his bad deeds, no longer mattered to him; his deeds were like a wave with its rippling effect, mattering only to the people on the shore who could not avoid getting their feet wet. And again, when I looked down at him, seeing him dead, I felt superior, I felt superior in the fact that I was alive and he was dead, and even though I knew and believed that death was my fate also, I felt superior to him, as if such a humiliation, death, would never happen to me. I was a child then, but you are a child until the people who brought you into this world are dead; you remain a child until you understand and believe that the people who brought you into this world are dead.

My father was buried. I do not know if he would have been amused by the absolute indifference with which his absence was met by the world he left behind.

I had been living at the end of the world for my whole life; it had been so when I was born, for my mother had died when I was born. But now, with my father dead, I was living at the brink of eternity, it was as if this quality of my life was suddenly raised from its usual self, embossed with its old meaning. The two people from whom I had come were no more. I had allowed no one to come from me. A new feeling of loneliness overcame me then; I grew agitated with a heat, then I grew still from a deep chill. I grew used to this loneliness, recognizing one day that in it were the things I had lost and the things I could have had but had refused. I came to love my father, but only when he was dead, at that moment when he still looked like himself but a self that could no longer cause harm, only a still self, dead; he was like a memory, not a picture, just a memory. And yet a memory cannot be trusted, for so much of the experience of the past is determined by the experience of the present.

To my wedding I wore a dress of pink faille silk. I wore around my neck a necklace of unpolished pearls that my father had given to me, a necklace that my sister and her mother did not want me to have; they said it had been lost, but on the day of my marriage they sent it to me. My husband and I did not make a joyful pair; we were very serious repeating the vows of loyalty until death should separate us. And the moment of our earthly union was so palpable, so certain, we could almost feel it with our hands.

My sister died. Her husband died. Her mother died. All the people I knew intimately from the beginning of my life died. I should have missed their presence but I did not.

I had never been sentimental. My life began with a wide panorama of possibilities: my birth itself was much like other births; I was new, the pages of my life had no writing on them, they were unsmudged, so clean, so smooth, so new. If I could have seen myself then, I could have imagined that my future would have filled volumes. Why should the world of adventure forever remain closed to me, the discovery of mountains, vast seas, miles upon miles of empty plains, the skies, the heavens, even the cruel subordination of others? Why should great acts of transgression be followed by profound redemption, a redemption of such magnitude that it had the power at once to make my own transgressions stomach-turning yet not unlike the naïve and simple actions of a child? Such was the case of a man who traded in human bodies and then wrote a hymn, a hymn of such fame that the descendants of the human bodies in which he had traded sang this hymn on Sundays in church with a fervor and sincerity that he, the author and transgressor, was not capable of. The depths of evil, its results, were all too clear to me: its satisfactions, its rewards, the glorious sensations, the praise, the feeling of exaltation and superiority evil elicits when it is successful, the feeling of invincibility—I had observed all of this firsthand. All roads come to an end, and all ends are the same, trailing off into nothing; even an echo eventually will be silenced.

I am of the vanquished, I am of the defeated. The past is a fixed point, the future is open-ended; for me the future must remain capable of casting a light on the past such that in my defeat lies the seed of my great victory, in my defeat lies the beginning of my great revenge. My impulse is to the good, my good is to serve myself. I am not a people, I am not a nation. I only wish from time to time to make my actions be the actions of a people, to make my actions be the actions of a nation.

I married a man I did not love. I did not do so on a whim, I did not do so after making a calculation, but this marriage had its usefulness. It allowed me to make a romance of my life, it allowed me to think of all my deeds and of myself with kindness in the deep dark of night, when sometimes it was necessary for me to do so. Romance is the refuge of the defeated; the defeated need songs to soothe themselves, they need a sweet tune to soothe themselves, for their whole being is a wound; they need a soft bed to sleep on, for when they are awake it is a nightmare, the dream of sleep is their reality. I married a man I did not love, but that word, "love," that idea, love—what could it mean to me, what should it mean to me? I did not know, and yet I would have saved him, I would have saved him from death, I would have saved him from a death I had not sanctioned myself, I would have saved him if ever he needed saving, as long as it was not from myself. Was this, then, a form of love, an incomplete love, or no love at all? I did not know. I believe my entire life was without such a thing, love, the kind of love you die from or the kind of love that causes you to live eternally, and if this was not actually so, I cannot be convinced of an otherwise.

And this man I married was of the victors, and so much a part of him was this situation, the situation of the conqueror, that only through a book of history could he be reminded of a time when he might have been something other, something like me, the vanquished, the defeated. When he looked at the night sky, it was closed off; so, too, was the midday sky, closed off; the seas were closed off, the ground on which he walked was closed off. He did not have a future, he had only the past, he lived in that way; it was not a past he was responsible for all by himself, it was a past he had inherited. He did not object to his inheritance; it was a good one, only it did not bring happiness; and his reply to such an assertion would be the correct one: What can bring happiness? At the moment the conqueror asks such a question, his defeat is secure. It was at such a moment in my husband's life that I met him, the moment when defeat, his own, that of the people he came from, was secure. I could say he loved me if I needed to hear I was loved, but I will never say it. He grew to live for the sound of my footsteps, so often I would walk without making a sound; he loved the sound of my voice, so for days I would not utter a word; I allowed him to touch me long after I could be moved by the touch of anyone.

He and I lived in this spell, the spell of history. I wore the color black, the color of mourners. I dressed him in the colors of the newly born, the innocent, the weak, youth: white, pale blue, pale yellow, and anything that had faded; these were not the colors of any flag. Each morning the great mountains covered in everlasting green faced us on one side, the great swath of gray seawater faced us on the other. The sky, the moon and stars and sun in that same sky—none of these things were under the spell of history, not his, not mine, not anybody's. Oh, to be a part of such a thing, to be a part of anything that is outside history, to be a part of something that can deny the wave of the human hand, the beat of the human heart, the gaze of the human eye, human desire itself. And each day he would walk along the perimeter of the land on which he lived; it would always remain strange to him, this land on which he had spent most of his life. He would stumble, he did not know its contours, the feel of it never became familiar to him; he was not born on it, he would only die on it and asked to be buried facing east, in the direction of the land in which he was born; he would stumble as he walked the perimeter, coming to a place where the land had split in two, a precipice, an abyss, but even that was closed to him, the abyss was closed to him. At the sight of him staring into a chasm in the earth, I was not moved with pity; no gesture that he made then, running his hands through his sparse hair, stroking his chin, wrapping his arms around his shoulders or around his torso, none of this moved me to consider his entire being in such a way that would make his suffering real to me. I was capable of doing so, of making his suffering real to myself, but I would not allow myself to do it.

He spoke to me, I spoke to him; he spoke to me in English, I spoke to him in patois. We understood each other much better that way, speaking to each other in the language of our thoughts. When he spoke to me his voice was soft, as if he, too, wanted to hear what it was he was saying. His voice was tender, sometimes it had the sound of a stream met unexpectedly in a place you could never forget. When I was young, when he first met me, when he did not know that my presence in his life was permanent, he liked the way my teeth glistened in strong light of any kind, he did everything possible to make me keep my mouth open; he made me sigh, he made me speak, but he could not make me laugh, not for him would I open my mouth in laughter. To see him eating a meal was always a revolting spectacle to me, but I long ago had learned to stop being surprised by this when I realized that many things which reminded me that he, too, was human and frail caused a great feeling of anger to swell up in me; for if he, too, was human, then would not all whom he came from be human, too, and where would that leave me and all that I came from?

He was not a man of any sophistication, a man of any accomplishment. He knew many things, but they were not from his own experience; he knew things that were a distillation of, condensed from, the experiences of many people, none of whom he knew, but I could not condemn him for this; how unusual is it to believe the beliefs—and even die for these beliefs—originating with people you can never and will never know? He was an heir, and like all such people the origin of his inheritance was a burden to him. He was not an ignorant man, he had a sense of justice, a sense of what might be right and what might be wrong. He was even a man of some courage; he could condemn himself. But to condemn yourself is to forgive yourself, and to forgive yourself for your transgressions against others is not a right that anybody can claim.

Before we were married and shortly after we were married, we lived in the capital of Dominica, Roseau. In places like Roseau, wars are fought, but there are no victories, only a standoff, only an until-next-time. We moved away from Roseau, in a state of mind, a calm, that was almost godlike, for it was beyond deliberation and beyond impulse. We moved to a place that was high above some mountains, but not at the top of the highest mountain. It was a place to rest. We were weary; we were weary of being ourselves, weary of our own legacies. He worshipped me, he loved me; that I did not require these things only increased the feelings he had for me. He thought I made him forget the past; he had no future, he wanted only to be in the present, each day was today, each moment this moment. But who can really forget the past? Not the victor, and not the vanquished, for even when words become forbidden, there are other ways to betray memory: the unmet eye; the wave of a hand that signifies the exact opposite of the friendly hello or the friendly goodbye. Or to sit in a chair in a room alone, believing yourself alone, allowing your spirit to hunt for a resting place and finding none (for there is no such thing, only in death, only a dreamless sleep) —this truth registers on the face, in the arrangement of the body itself.

Who can forget? This man I lived with for many years, and whom I would live without for a long time after that, would gather around him various things. In his life, by his tradition, he had become convinced of a certain truth, and this truth was based on reducing, so that only what survived was deemed worthy. He and all like him had survived, so far. He looked at the land on which he lived, he made decisions, his decisions were limited to what pleased him, his idea of what might be beautiful, and then what was beautiful. He cleared the land; nothing growing on it inspired any interest in him. The inflorescence of this, he said, was not significant; and the word "inflorescence" was said with an authority, as if he had created inflorescence itself, which made me laugh with such pleasure I lost consciousness for that moment of my own existence. He took sheets of glass and, gluing them together, made boxes in which he would place a lizard, a crab whose habitat was the land—not the sea, not both, only the land; in a box made of glass he placed a turtle whose habitat was the land, not the sea, not both, only the land; in a box made of glass he placed small frog after small frog; they died, frozen in that pose of stillness natural to a frog which is meant to confound a foe. He made long lists under the heading Genus, he made long lists under the heading Species. From time to time I would release whatever individual he held in captivity, replacing it with its like, its kind: one lizard replaced with another lizard, one crab replaced with another crab, one frog with another frog; I could not ever tell if he knew I had done so. He was so sure inside himself that all the things he knew were correct, not that they were true, but that they were correct. Truth would have undone him, the truth is always so full of uncertainty.

And when finally I was a true orphan, my father had at last died and he died not knowing me, not ever speaking to me in a language in which I could have faith, a language in which I could believe the things he said—when I was a true orphan then, the reality of how alone I had been in the world, how I would become even more so, brought me an air of peace. My entire life so far, all seventy years of it, I had dreaded the moment when I would be alone; the two people I had come from, the two people who had made me, dead; but then at last a great peace came over me, a quietness that was not silence and not acceptance, just a feeling of peace, a resolve. I was alone and I was not afraid, I accepted it the way I accepted all the things that were true of me: my two hands, my two eyes, my two feet, my two ears, all my senses, all that could be known about me, all that I did not know. That I was alone was now a true thing. This fact did not have a codicil attached, a metaphorical asterisk was not a part of this statement. There was no aside. I was alone in the world.

The man to whom I was married, my husband, was alone, too, but he did not accept it, he did not have the strength to do so. He drew on the noisiness of the world into which he was born, conquests, the successful disruption of other peoples' worlds, peoples whose reality he and those he came from could not understand, so instead of bowing before such an incomprehensibility lifted up their heads and committed murder. He now busied himself with the dead, arranging, disarranging, rearranging the books on his shelf, volumes of history, geography, science, philosophy, speculations: none of it could bring him peace. He now lived in a world in which he could not speak the language. I mediated for him, I translated for him. I did not always tell him the truth, I did not always tell him everything. I blocked his entrance to the world in which he lived; eventually I blocked his entrance into all the worlds he had come to know. He became all the children I did not allow to be born, some of them fathered by him, some of them fathered by others. I would oversee his end also. I gave him a kind and sweet burial, even though it could not matter to him. What makes the world turn? He never needed an answer to such a question.

Did so much sadness ever enclose two people? Yet not the same kind of sadness, for it did not come from the same source, this sadness. His life, the external part of it, was full of victories, hardly a desire that could not be fulfilled, and the power to make the world the way he wished it to be. And yet—oh, and yet—how is it possible to be so lost? There are many ways to be lost. All ways are ways to be lost. So how much pity should I extend to him? Could he be blamed for believing that the successful actions of his ancestors bestowed on him the right to act in an unprecedented, all-powerful way, and without consequences? He believed in a race, he believed in a nation, he believed in all this so completely that he could step outside it; he wanted at the end of his life only to die with me, though I was not his race, I was not of his nation.

Who was I? My mother died at the moment I was born. You are not yet anything at the moment you are born. This fact of my mother dying at the moment I was born became a central motif of my life. I cannot remember when I first knew this fact of my life, I cannot remember when I did not know this fact of my life; perhaps it was at the moment I could recognize my own hand, and then again there was never a moment that I can remember when I did not know myself completely. My body now is still; when it moves, it moves inward, shrinking into itself, withering like fruit dying on a vine, not rotting like fruit that has been picked and lies uneaten on a dirty plate. For years and years, each month my body would swell up slightly, mimicking the state of maternity, longing to conceive, mourning my heart's and mind's decision never to bring forth a child. I refused to belong to a race, I refused to accept a nation. I wanted only, and still do want, to observe the people who do so. The crime of these identities, which I know now more than ever, I do not have the courage to bear. Am I nothing, then? I do not believe so, but if nothing is a condemnation, then I would love to be condemned.

I can hear the sound of much emptiness now. A shift of my head this way to the right, that way to the left; I hear it, a soft rushing sound, waiting to grow bigger, waiting to envelop me. It holds no fear, only a growing curiosity. I only wish to know it so that I may one day tell myself the story of my existence within it. It is not an amusement. To know all is an impossibility, but only such a thing would satisfy me. To reverse the past would bring me complete happiness. Such an event—for it would be that, an event—would make my world stand on its feet; it does so now and has for a long time stood on its head. In a moment of extreme recklessness, I once said this to my husband—recklessness because to allow him an entry into my deepest thoughts was to give him a small measure of understanding of me. I once said to him that I was born standing on my head, the world then was upside down at the moment I first laid eyes on it, and he said, with a laugh, that everybody came into the world that way. I was not everybody, and it pleased me to know he did not understand this. He laughed when he told me this, I laughed when he told me this. When he laughed, his face opened with pleasure, grew wide as if about to split; but when he saw my own pleasure in his pleasure, he understood his mistake; we could not both be happy at the same time. Life, History, whatever its name, had made such a thing an impossibility. He never grew grim, there were no hardships in his own life, his disappointments were not known to him. His life grew darker, its opening was closing up. Seeing him in that way, standing at the edge of a cliff that faced east, the direction in which he would be buried, standing there on its very edge, precariously yet soundly balanced, like a bird, not a bird of prey but the humble winged being that inspires love and fantasy in children, I wanted to push him over, into the abyss, and not with deliberate anger but with a tap-tap, as if of recognition, as if of a friend, as if to say to him, You were not the great love of my life and so I understand you completely and this sentiment is unusual, unique only to me. Ahhh!

This account of my life has been an account of my mother's life as much as it has been an account of mine, and even so, again it is an account of the life of the children I did not have, as it is their account of me. In me is the voice I never heard, the face I never saw, the being I came from. In me are the voices that should have come out of me, the faces I never allowed to form, the eyes I never allowed to see me. This account is an account of the person who was never allowed to be and an account of the person I did not allow myself to become.

The days are long, the days are short. The nights are a blank; they harken to something, but I refuse to become familiar with it. To that period of time called day I profess an indifference; such a thing is a vanity but known only to me; all that is impersonal I have made personal. Since I do not matter, I do not long to matter, but I matter anyway. I long to meet the thing greater than I am, the thing to which I can submit. It is not in a book of history, it is not the work of anyone whose name can pass my own lips. Death is the only reality, for it is the only certainty, inevitable to all things.